MARGARE

hanging
on to max

Simon Pulse
New York London Toronto Sydney Singapore

Dedicated to the memory of my mother, Catherine Bechard

First Simon Pulse edition December 2003
Copyright © 2002 by Margaret Bechard

SIMON PULSE
An imprint of Simon & Schuster Children's Publishing Division
1230 Avenue of the Americas, New York, NY 10020

First published in the United States by Roaring Brook Press,
a division of Millbrook Press, in 2002

Designed by Lisa Vega
The text of this book was set in Janson Text.
Printed in the United States of America
                15 16 17 18 19 20

The Library of Congress has cataloged the hardcover edition as follows:
Bechard, Margaret.
Hanging on to Max / Margaret Bechard
p. cm.
Summary: When his girlfriend decides to give their baby away, seventeen-year-old Sam is
determined to keep him and raise him alone.
[1. Teenage parents—Fiction. 2. Teenage fathers—Fiction. 3. Fathers and sons—Fiction]
I. Title
PZ7.B380655 Han 2002
[Fic]—dc21   2001048335
ISBN 0-7613-1579-9 (hc)
ISBN 0-7613-2574-3 (library binding)
ISBN-13: 978-0-689-86268-7 (Simon Pulse pbk.)
ISBN-10: 0-689-86268-7 (Simon Pulse pbk.)

chapter one

THE TOTAL SILENCE WOKE me up. I opened my eyes, slowly, and there they all were, watching me. Ms. Garcia, with her sad little worn-out smile. The rest of the class, grinning like monkeys. The room was almost dark, except for the light from the slide projector.

"Nice nap, Sam?" Ms. Garcia asked. Everyone burst out laughing. Ooh. Good one, Ms. Garcia. Except what teacher in her right mind would turn out the lights and show slides at 1:30 in the afternoon?

I shrugged upright in my desk. "Sorry." I shook my head, trying to clear it out.

"Do you know what this slide is, Sam?"

I squinted at the screen. "Jupiter?"

People applauded. Someone in the back whistled. I

rubbed my eyes. When I'd fallen asleep, there'd been a slide of a woman making cookies. Ms. Garcia's "Why We Should Study Math" inspirational slide show.

"Okay," Ms. Garcia said, "in 1995 NASA sent a probe from the Galileo spacecraft down through the atmosphere of Jupiter." The slide projector clunked to a picture of the probe.

"It looks like a giant tit," some guy said.

Ms. Garcia sighed. "Okay. Well. The probe sent back a stream of data for 57.6 minutes, until the incredible pressure of the Jovian atmosphere crushed it."

"Poor little probe," the girl next to me said.

"Bor-ing," somebody in back said.

I imagined the probe, analyzing, computing, while the weight of Jupiter pressed in heavier and heavier.

"So," Ms. Garcia said, "do you think the scientists at NASA had to use math to design this probe? And to communicate with it?"

"I'd rather design a giant tit," the guy in back said.

Ms. Garcia sighed. The next slide was a Volvo. "Now back on Earth the safety engineers . . ."

I put my head back down on the desk and closed my eyes.

MARGARET BECHARD

The bell woke me up. Kids were grabbing books and papers, cramming them into backpacks. Everybody talking at once. At the front of the room, Ms. Garcia was saying something about turning in the test papers from the beginning of class and something that was due next Wednesday. But nobody was listening. People were jamming up in the doorway, pushing to get out. "Test papers," Ms. Garcia said again.

The guy who sat behind me, who always smelled faintly of sweat and cigarette smoke, slapped my back. "Hey, dude. At least you weren't drooling."

"Right," I said. "Thanks." I stared down at my test. I'd finished it in the first ten minutes. And that had included checking my answers three times. I stood up slowly and shrugged into my backpack.

As I dropped the paper on her desk, Ms. Garcia's hand snaked out and grabbed my wrist. "Give me a couple of minutes, please, Sam?"

I glanced at the clock. "It's 2:30."

"They'll wait for you."

I sighed and moved out of the flow of kids. Good job, Sam. Two weeks into September and already you've ticked her off. Already you're blowing this. A kid stopped to explain why he'd done only the first three problems on the test. And then Marcella went into a long thing about how she was going to Mexico for two weeks and needed to know what she'd miss. I shuffled around a little, banged my foot against the garbage can, just to let them know I was still standing there, but nobody paid any attention.

Finally the last kid left. Ms. Garcia ran her fingers through her hair. Her face was tense, like maybe she had a bad headache.

"I've really gotta go, Ms. Garcia." I pointed to the clock. "And I'm sorry about falling asleep. It's just . . . we had a bad night last night. I didn't . . ."

She waved her hand. "I know. I know. Everybody had a bad night last night." She leaned toward me. "The real problem here, Sam, is you don't belong in this class."

I took a breath. "But this is the only math class that fits in my schedule. We went through this whole thing, Mrs. Harriman and me." Besides, I liked this class. I needed an easy class. I took another breath, deeper, slower. Don't panic here, Sam. Get a grip. "I need the credit. I *have* to graduate this year."

Ms. Garcia tilted her head to one side and looked up

at me. "I talked to Mr. Wright, Sam, yesterday. Your math teacher at Willamette View?"

I nodded. Mr. Wright. He'd been okay. Andy had called him "Mr. Wrong," which was pretty dumb, but I'd always laughed, because it was Andy.

"Mr. Wright loaned me a different text. It comes with a computer program. It'll let you work at your own speed."

I laughed. My own speed? My own speed was like a dead stop. "You know, Ms. Garcia, I sort of dropped out of Mr. Wright's class."

"But he says you had a good grasp of all the concepts. A very good grasp, he told me." She pointed to the iMac in the corner. "We can set you up over there. You can work on the computer in class and take the textbook home with you." She held it up, barely. It looked like it weighed about 500 pounds. "It actually gets into precalculus."

I could tell she wanted me to be impressed, excited. "But . . . " I started.

"And if you get stuck, I can help you out. I was a math major, you know." She smiled at me, her eyes big behind her wire-framed glasses. "I'm not saying it won't be hard work, Sam. But don't just say no. At least think about it." And her smile widened, a little desperate looking. Ms. Garcia, the math major, teaching bonehead math in an alternative high school. "I don't want to lose you, Sam. I think, if you were challenged more, you might sleep a little less."

And who needed sleep? I took another breath. If it would make her happy, if I could stay in her class, if I could graduate like I was supposed to, what was one more thing? "Sure," I said. "Sure. I can give it a try." I took the book. It did weigh 500 pounds.

She nodded, once. "Good. I'm glad, Sam. I don't think you'll regret this."

It took me five minutes to get to my locker. The halls were packed with kids, goofing around, laughing, yelling. Typical end-of-the-day high.

I jerked my locker open. It smelled funny. Gym socks? Rotting sandwich? I didn't have time to figure it out. I grabbed my English book and the stack of government worksheets. I stuffed them all into my backpack and slammed my locker shut.

The secretary looked up from her monitor as I burst through the day care doors. "We'd about given up on you," she said, but she was smiling. They all smiled at me, all the time.

"I had to talk to Ms. Garcia," I said. I shouldered through the door into the crawlers room.

"Here he is!" Mrs. McPherson, the teacher, said. "Here's Daddy."

Max leaned out of her arms toward me, his hands stretched out, his face red and swollen with crying.

I took him. "Hey, buddy. It's okay." He wrapped his arms around my neck, taking a big hiccuppy breath, twining his fingers into the long hairs at the back of my neck. I patted him gently. "Let's go home."

chapter two

I WAS ALMOST ALL the way home when I remembered we were out of diapers. So I had to double back all the way to the Safeway up on Barbur. Max had fallen asleep in his car seat, and it would have been a whole lot easier to just leave him, but I knew I couldn't do that.

He woke up as soon as I lifted him out. I held my breath, thinking maybe he was going to start screaming again. You never knew. But he just grinned up at me, and when I put him in the seat of the shopping cart, he made this goofy little squealy noise. Max got off on grocery stores.

I hated grocery stores. I hated the way people stared at us.

I went straight to the baby aisle and grabbed a giant

MARGARET BECHARD

pack of diapers. And some of the wipey things. We were probably out of those, too. I should have made a list. Dumb, Sam. I threw in a can of formula, just in case. I was keeping a running tally in my head. The Datsun needed gas, and I only had like twenty-five bucks left from the money Dad had given me on Sunday.

I headed out of the aisle and saw Martha Bennett's mother coming out of the produce section. I couldn't believe it. I'd picked this store because it was so far from home. I skidded the cart to a stop. Martha and I had played on the same indoor soccer team all through elementary school. I did not want to talk to her mother. I knew the look she'd give me. I knew just how she'd say, "Oh, Sam. How *are* you, Sam?"

I whipped into the next aisle, Max grabbing the bar in front of him and laughing. "Shh," I hissed. "Shh." We were in snack food. I grabbed a bag of Cheez Puffs and pretended to be reading the back, just in case she came down this aisle.

Cheez Puffs. I turned the bag over in my hands. Andy and I had lived on these things, weekends at his house. I used to spend just about every Friday night at Andy's, back in elementary and middle school.

Max leaned out of the cart, snagged a cardboard display of dip and nearly dragged it over.

I grabbed it just before all the little cans hit the floor. "Max!"

"Woo-woo!" he said. He grinned at me. I tossed the Cheez Puffs back on the shelf.

I peered around the end of the aisle. Mrs. Bennett was nowhere in sight, so I made a dash for the express line.

The checker smiled at Max. "Aren't you a sweetheart?" she said.

Max leaned over and blew a big spit bubble at her.

"Isn't he precious?" She reached over and tweaked Max's cheek. Then she looked up at me. "Is this your little brother?"

I nodded.

"And you're helping your mom out?"

I nodded again.

"Well." She gave Max another tweak, and he squealed. "Your mother must be very proud of both of you."

When we got home, I thought about sticking Max in his high chair, with a bottle and some crackers. Or maybe even sticking him in his crib. Just while I tried to get something done. I had about a million things to do.

MARGARET BECHARD

But playing with Max was one of the things I was supposed to do. It was on the list on the wall in my bedroom.

I took him into the living room and put him on the floor. I put Metallica on the CD player. A classic. The parenting book said music was good for a baby's mental development.

We played chase the baby around the living room, both of us crawling, Max shrieking and laughing. It was cool, to make him so crazy happy. We sat for a minute, beside the couch, both of us panting and grinning. "Ready to go again, buddy?" I asked.

He blinked at me, and he gave me a look, a look he had sometimes. Like he knew something I didn't know. And then, all of a sudden, he crawled under the coffee table, stretched out flat, and, in about ten seconds, fell fast asleep.

I sat there, watching him, making sure this was for real, making sure he wasn't just going to pop back up again. But he was out cold. "Yes!" I whispered. I clicked off the CD, lay down on the rug beside him, and I fell asleep, too.

Dad coming into the kitchen at 5:30 woke me up. My first thought was, Oh hell, where's Max? Nobody had ever specifically said it, but falling asleep like that was probably bad, too. Only he was still conked under the table.

Dad came into the doorway and looked at us.

"Hey," I said, quietly.

"I brought home Chinese food. Let's eat quick before he wakes up."

I scrambled to my feet. "Sounds great." And it did. It sounded wonderful. I hadn't had anything to eat since the gluey cafeteria macaroni at 11:30.

I filled my plate with lo mein and fried shrimp and kung pao chicken. Dad ate the way he always does—one thing at a time. First the shrimp. Then the chicken. He even ate his rice separately, at the very end. When he was done, he set his fork down on his empty plate. "Has your Aunt Jean called?"

I was digging for the last of the noodles. "Not yet."

When it had seemed like maybe they wouldn't give me custody, because Mom was dead, and it was just Dad and me, Aunt Jean had stepped up. Had said she'd be here. And she had been. She'd moved in with us in December, and then stayed through January and February and March. It had been great. Max was so tiny, just a worm baby. I was totally clueless. Aunt Jean had known everything. How to change diapers, mix formula, get him to sleep. It had been kind of a shock when she'd said she thought I had the hang of it, and it was time for her to go back and look after Uncle Ted. A shock for both Dad and me.

"She'll call tonight," I said. "She always calls on Wednesdays." I dumped the leftover rice into the leftover kung pao and mixed it around in the box.

Dad nodded. He waited until I'd eaten the last grain of rice, then took the empty box from me. I slumped back in my chair. I knew I should get Max up. He'd never sleep tonight if he napped like this now. But I couldn't move.

Dad tossed all the boxes in the garbage. Then he filled a glass with water and drank it, standing by the sink.

"So," I said. "How was work?"

He put the glass down. "Okay."

I nodded. "Still wiring that building in Tualatin?"

"That's right. School okay?"

"Fine."

He nodded. He pointed with his chin toward the living room. "He's okay?"

"He's great."

Dad nodded again. Then he glanced up at the clock on the microwave. "I want to catch SportsCenter." He looked back at me. "Is there anything . . . " He looked around the kitchen, like there was something he might find. "Is there anything you need?"

I frowned. For a second, all I could think of were things I needed. But I gave him a big smile. "Nope," I said. "I've got it all under control."

He nodded. "Good then." And he went out of the kitchen. A few seconds later, I heard the TV in his bedroom click on.

I sat there, staring at the plates, shiny with grease and soy sauce. Something to add to the list: Never, ever make Max feel like he's disappointed you in some big unfixable forever way. And then, just a flash, I tried to imagine Max in seventeen years. Me and Max. I shook my head. I couldn't even imagine Max in seventeen minutes.

I hauled myself up out of the chair. I had to clean Max's bottles, get them ready for tomorrow. And wash the plates and forks Dad and I had just used. Do some laundry. Max was out of clean clothes again.

Homework. A ton and a half of homework.

MARGARET BECHARD

I was rinsing the last bottle when the phone rang. "Hello?"

"Hey, Sam." There was silence, then, "It's me. Andy. Andy Pederson," he added.

"Andy? Andy! I . . . hey, man." I nearly said, I was just thinking about you today. I nearly told him about the Cheez Puffs. But that would sound stupid. "How's it going?"

"It's going . . . it's good, dude. Listen. I just wanted . . ." He paused, and I could picture him, sitting there, his feet jigging up and down. Andy was a high-energy kind of guy. "Listen. I made varsity, you know."

I didn't know. "No kidding! Way to go!"

"Yeah. Finally, huh? My senior year. Perfect timing."

We were both quiet. And I knew he was remembering all the times we'd talked about being seniors. Back when we were little pitiful freshmen. How great it would be to be seniors together. How maybe we'd even go to the same college. I could feel the memories, clogging the phone lines.

And suddenly I realized that, actually, I was a little ticked. Andy hadn't called me in like six months. He'd come over once, which had been sort of a disaster. Max had been sick. But he called me now, to tell me his great news. "Varsity," I said.

"The thing is, we're playing a home game? This Friday? And I thought you might . . . well . . . it should be a good game. And, I mean, you know, you can bring the baby."

In the living room, Max grunted. He was awake. Awake and filling his pants. "Hey, Andy. Dude. I'm glad you called."

"Do you think you can make it? To the game?"

"I'll think about it. This Friday." Max had stopped grunting and was starting to whimper.

"But, listen. Sam . . ."

I hung up before he could finish.

chapter three

I KNOW WHAT THEY say about teenage boys. Every eight seconds. That's how often we think about sex.

But I am not thinking about sex that night in December. Not me and sex, anyway.

Andy calls around 8:00. I'm sitting in the living room, flicking through the channels. Dad's gone to the Blazer game.

Andy says, "Hey, man. Want to go to a party?"

I click to wrestling. Back to MTV. "Where?"

"Melissa Talbot's."

I groan, which Andy is expecting, because he says, right away, "Come on, Sam. I know you're not doing anything."

"I'm very busy." I click to VH1.

"You're sitting in front of the tube. I know how you like to spend Friday nights."

I click to Comedy Central. Andy and I are sophomores now. I never spend Friday nights at his place anymore. Not since he started going out with Jenny, last spring. Especially not since I'd met Brittany Ames.

"Jenny's friends suck," I say.

"Yeah. Well." Andy sighs. "Look. I don't want you to come to this party for me. I want you to come for *you*."

I laugh. He sounds like Mr. Rutger in our careers class. There's a sitcom on channel four. The teenage witch thing.

"You can't mope around about Brittany forever."

"Just shut up, okay, Andy?"

He does, for about two seconds. "What was this fight about again?"

I click fast past a deodorant commercial, a cowboy movie, stop on a cooking show. "She just started yelling at me. I mean it, man. I didn't do anything." This is true. This was our first fight since we'd started going out in October. Maybe I had said something. Maybe I had done something. Or hadn't done something?

"And you've tried to talk to her?"

"Yes. Of course." This is a lie.

Andy sighs, a wet, blubbery noise against the mouthpiece. "Jenny says maybe you should apologize."

I nearly drop the remote. "What? I'm not apologizing when I didn't even do anything." When she hasn't even tried to talk to me.

"Okay. Okay." Andy's quiet again. The guy on the TV is frying onions, and I realize I'm hungry. "It's been a week, right?"

"Six days."

"Six days? Six days!" His voice is so loud, I have to move the receiver away from my ear. "That's it, Sam. Time's up. Time to get a life. Time . . ." His voice deepens, lowers. "Time to party."

"At Melissa Talbot's," I say. "Hold me back." I click back to the teenage witch, who is kind of hot.

"Jenny thinks Claire Bailey will be there."

"Claire Bailey?" I try to say it like I'm not exactly sure who that is. Claire Bailey? Hmm. Doesn't ring a bell.

"Claire Bailey?" Andy says, in exactly the same tone of voice. Then he laughs. "You're so lame, Pettigrew. You're so hopeless. You've loved her since the sixth grade."

"Oh, yeah. Right." A cop show on channel eight. I haven't loved her. I've just been . . . interested. "What time are you and Jenny going?"

"Around nine."

Claire Bailey. Not that we remotely had anything in common. Not anything like me and Brittany. "I'll think about it," I say. "If there's nothing on TV."

When I get to Melissa's, around 9:15, Andy and Jenny aren't there. I wander from room to room, checking out the crowd. Claire Bailey isn't there, either.

But Brittany is. She's standing in the kitchen, trying to open a bottle of root beer—one of those expensive kinds—the top is supposed to twist off. Brittany can never open those.

I stop in the doorway, because I don't want her to think I've been looking for her. I don't want her to think I'm so desperate I'm following her around to stupid parties. But then she looks at me, and I don't care what she thinks. I just want it to be like it was before. "Here. Let me do it," I say. And I open the root beer for her.

As I hand it back to her, we both say, at exactly the same time, "I'm sorry."

And then we both laugh.

MARGARET BECHARD

And it feels so good, it feels so good to have Brittany not mad anymore, it's like the last six days didn't even happen. "I got that Weezer CD," I say. "The one I was talking about?"

"Is it great?"

"Yeah. Yeah, it really is. There's not a bad track. Every song's good."

Two guys are rummaging in the refrigerator, and a girl in the corner is talking on a cell phone. A burst of noise rolls in from the living room.

Brittany steps a little closer. I can smell the root beer on her breath. "Could we go over to your house and listen to it?"

"Sure," I say.

We go out to my car. And I know nobody will believe this, but I am not thinking about sex. All I'm thinking is how glad I am she's back, sitting in my car, messing with the radio, turning the heat up too high. And I'm thinking how I can't wait to tell Andy.

Nobody's home, of course. In the last two months, we've gone to Brittany's house lots of times. This is the first time we've gone to my house. Brittany looks around the living room and she says, "Nice house." And it is nice. I mean, it's just Dad and me, but the house always looks good. Dad has this thing about neatness. And now I'm sort of proud, proud of us.

"The CDs in my room," I say, and we go on back. And I'm thinking about the CD, about where I'd put it. And whether I'd picked up my underwear that morning.

My room looks good, too. No underwear and Weezer's right on my desk. Brittany sits on the bed, and I start the CD. I sit down beside her. We sit there for a while, listening to the music. She's singing along, under her breath. Then she turns to me and I see there are tears in her eyes. "I missed you so much," she says, and she puts her hand on my leg. "I love you, Sam."

I take a very deep breath. I'm really afraid to open my mouth, afraid whatever I say, it'll be the wrong thing. Because now, well, okay, now I *am* thinking about sex. Actually, I've been thinking about it since the beginning of the last song. So I lean over, and I kiss her, and she kisses me back.

And that's when I pretty much stop thinking anything at all.

MARGARET BECHARD

chapterfour

MAX DIDN'T FALL ASLEEP again until 11:00. The list above my desk said, "Get Max to sleep by 9:00." Right under "Drink out of a cup" and "nap schedule." I couldn't even remember what "nap schedule" meant.

I spent the next two hours in the kitchen, trying to work on the English paper. I wrote half a paragraph.

Max woke up, like always, at 5:30. I didn't need an alarm clock anymore, not with Max around.

He fell asleep on the way to school, so I carried him in still in his car seat. The metal detectors were set up at the front door. They were supposed to rotate them around all the middle schools and the high schools in the district, but they were almost always at the alternative school.

I carried Max through. The car seat set off the buzzer. The car seat always set off the buzzer. Max jerked, but he didn't wake up.

"It's the car seat," I said to the security guy.

He looked me up and down and shook his head. "We gotta check." He nodded me over to the table where his partner, who looked exactly like Elmer Fudd in a uniform, started going through my backpack and the diaper bag. "It's the car seat," I said, hoping they didn't wake up Max. The guy grunted and pulled out diapers and Max's favorite blanket and my government worksheets. I could tell what he was thinking. "Damn teenagers. Damn teenagers screwing around." I took a deep breath.

The front door opened, and Brianna walked in carrying Fox in his car seat. Her two-year-old, Callie, was hanging onto her pant leg. Callie was eating a banana.

Brianna walked through the metal detector. It buzzed. Max startled and woke up. "It's the car seat," Brianna said, smiling.

"Go right on through," the security guy said. He smiled down at Callie. "You eat up your banana now, sweetheart."

Max started to cry. "Step back," Elmer Fudd said to me. "I have to go over you with the handheld."

I closed my eyes and started counting to 1,000 by 3's.

When I got to the day care, Christy and Meredith were in the corner, talking. Christy had Tyler on her hip. Tawna was sitting in the rocking chair, nursing Kylie. "Sam and Max," she said, like it was one word. "What's wrong with Max?"

"He wants out." I unstrapped him from the seat. He screamed louder.

"He's probably hungry," Meredith said.

"Or sick," Christy said. "Does he have an ear infection?"

"Probably needs a new diaper," Tawna said, like I would never, ever think of that myself. "Have you checked his diaper, Sam?"

Mrs. McPherson came in. "What's wrong, Max?" She held out her hands and took him. He stopped crying, right away. I saw Christy and Meredith exchange smiles.

Mrs. McPherson looked at me. "And what's wrong with Sam?"

I'm sick and tired of everybody knowing what I should be doing. "They wouldn't let me through the metal detector again," I said. "They let Brianna through, no problem."

Mrs. McPherson sighed and patted Max.

"It's not fair," I said. I knew I sounded whiny and stupid, and I knew fathers probably weren't supposed to talk like that, but I couldn't help it.

"I'll mention it to them." Mrs. McPherson patted me, too. "Make sure you put extra diapers in the changing room today, okay? You forgot yesterday."

Nicole and Tawna and Gemma came in with their kids, and two of the volunteers walked in with them. "Get organized, people," Mrs. McPherson said. "You don't want to be late for class." She handed Max to one of the volunteers. He gave her a big grin.

I grabbed his diapers for the day, checked I'd labeled them all with his name, and headed for the changing room. Some of the babies—most of the babies—this age cried when their moms left. Max didn't even seem to notice I was gone.

As I rounded the corner, I ran smack into some idiot standing in the middle of the hall.

"Hey," I said. "Watch . . ."

It was Claire Bailey. Claire Bailey. Long floaty dark hair. Big brown eyes. Came just up to my chin. Claire Bailey.

"Sam Pettigrew! I heard you were here." She was holding a baby, one of the little ones, from the newborn room.

I felt my face get hot. "Yeah. Well." I tried to shift around her. Claire was probably here for community service. Or some kind of class project. Something that would look good on her college applications.

She pulled the blanket back from the baby's face. "This is Emily. Isn't she beautiful?"

Emily was a tiny baby. Not very old. Her head was red and scaly where it wasn't covered in wispy black hair. Her nose was flattened against her face and her lips were kind of squooshed together. Her cheeks were covered in little red zits. "Whoa," I said. "She can only get better."

Claire looked at me and down at the baby and back at me. And I realized two things. This was *her* baby. And she'd been crying.

"I mean, she *can't* get any better. Can she? I mean, she's pretty cute."

But Claire wasn't paying any attention. She folded the blanket back over Emily's face. "This is our first day," Claire said. And her eyes filled with tears. "It'll be my first day away from her."

"Ah."

"I just hate to miss anything, you know?" She looked at me. The tears were starting to flood out, onto her cheeks.

"Ah," I said again.

Claire gave a choked up sort of sob, and then she really started crying, her body shaking, Emily shaking. Emily's eyelids fluttered and opened, and she gave a little mewing wail.

I stuck Max's diapers under my arm. "Here," I said. "Let me take her. You don't want to drop her."

Claire's eyes widened, like she hadn't thought of that. Then she handed Emily over. She slumped against the wall, still sobbing. The little rings running up her right ear quivered.

I tucked Emily into the crook of my arm and jiggled her up and down. It seemed like Max had never been this little.

Claire sucked back tears. She took a shaky breath. "Where's your baby?"

I pointed with my head. "In the crawler room." I jiggled Emily some more. "You know. This is a good place. She'll be okay."

Claire started crying again. "I know," she sobbed.

"And the thing about missing stuff," I plowed on, even though I just seemed to be making things worse. "Christy? She's another mom. She's always leaving class to check on Tyler. Like he's going to do something amazing while she's in keyboarding?" I leaned closer and lowered my voice. "Only Tyler's a lump. Tyler never does anything."

Claire sobbed again. I wished I could just hand her a Ritz cracker or a bottle or something. "I'm not saying Emily's a lump," I said. I looked down at her. She was exactly a lump. "She's really . . . I mean . . . "

Claire snorted back tears and waved a hand at me. And I realized she was laughing now. "Stop, stop. This is way too comforting." She dug in the diaper bag at her feet, pulled out a spit-up rag, and wiped it across her face.

"Gross," I said.

She looked at it and tossed it back in the bag. She held out her arms. "Give me my lumpy baby." And she grinned.

I handed Emily over. "They get less lumpy. In a month or so."

"Unless they're Tyler." Claire raised her eyebrows.

"Right. Tyler will be a lump when's he's sixteen." And we both laughed.

Claire took another breath, not so shaky this time. "I keep thinking, if I could only get some sleep."

I nodded, then I snapped my fingers. "Wait a minute. Are you taking government?"

"Third period."

"Perfect. A fifty-minute nap, right there. And just before lunch."

She grinned again. "I'll put it in my planner." She pulled Emily tighter against her and picked up the diaper bag. "I gotta feed her. Wish us luck. Me and the lump."

"You'll both be fine."

Nicole and Meredith came out of the crawler room, armed with diapers and wipes and extra clothes. Damn. I'd forgotten extra clothes again.

"Who was that?" Meredith asked, nodding toward Claire disappearing into the newborn room.

"New mom," I said.

"Boy or girl?" Nicole asked.

"Girl."

"She still needs to lose about ten pounds," Meredith said. Meredith was wearing a tight white blouse and a pair of low-riding black jeans. Andy would say she was hot. "I started exercising the day Mykala was born," Meredith said.

"You can't just eat and eat," Nicole said, as if Claire had been standing there eating a Big Mac or something. "And you can't wear sweatpants forever."

I wanted to say that Nicole was wearing sweatpants. I wanted to say that Claire had looked okay to me. But I didn't.

Nicole pointed to Max's diapers, still under my arm. "You know, Sam, you can get cheaper ones at Target."

"And they're so cute," Meredith said. She held up hers. "See. Baby ducks."

"Cute." I couldn't even buy friggin' diapers right.

They both laughed again and pushed past me to the changing room.

I just stood there, staring at the door of the newborn room. Claire Bailey. Claire Bailey was going to school here. I took a deep breath. I felt better than I had in a long time.

chapter five

CLAIRE BAILEY IS IN my eighth grade English class. We've just finished reading *To Kill a Mockingbird*, and Mrs. Perris is giving us our final assignment. "I want you to ask some adult," Mrs. Perris says, "a parent, a grandparent, an aunt or uncle, a neighbor . . ."

"The guy at the video store," Andy says. "The guy at the gas station."

Everybody laughs. Mrs. Perris frowns.

"An adult you respect," she says, before Andy can get going again. "I want you to ask this adult about some moment in their lives that they see as a turning point . . ." Hands are going up, so she adds, quickly, ". . . a moment in their lives that changed them, that made them see things differently, that maybe made them live their lives differently."

Andy looks at me and makes a gagging sound. I slump down in my desk. "How long?" Andy asks.

"A whole page. Double spaced. *One*-inch margins, please," Mrs. Perris says, and she points at Andy. Everybody laughs.

That night, at dinner, I ask Dad. Not because I'm all hot to do this paper. It's not due for like a week or something. But we're sitting there, eating our spaghetti. We've already done the "How was your day? Okay. Have any homework? Some." conversation. And now it's so quiet I can hear the little tick-tick noise the furnace makes just before it kicks on, way down in the basement. So, all of a sudden, I don't know, maybe just to block out the ticking, I say, "We have this English assignment. This essay thing. I'm supposed to ask you about some moment in your life that changed you forever."

And he doesn't miss a beat. He doesn't even stop eating. He says, "The day I met your mother." And he keeps on chewing.

I just sit there. Because Mom died when I was nine.

And now I'm thirteen. And in those four years, Dad has never mentioned her to me. Not once. And now, all of a sudden, while we're sitting here eating spaghetti—and for a second, all I can think of is how much I miss her and how much I wish she was here with us.

I watch him scrape at the last bite on his plate. I can't push any words past the lump in my throat. I can't ask him what he means. "The day I met your mother." And I know I can never write a paper about this.

But the next day, Claire comes to class, and she raises her hand, and she says, "I don't think we should have to do this assignment. The turning point thing."

Most kids, if they said something like that, the teacher would just ignore them, or say something like, "Well, too bad. Do it anyway."

But Mrs. Perris likes Claire. A lot. Claire loves to discuss things. Mrs. Perris and Claire discuss things all the time.

So now Mrs. Perris perches her butt on the edge of her desk and she says, "Why don't you think you should have to do this assignment, Claire?"

Everyone in the class is sitting up and paying attention. This is a good discussion. I am paying total attention.

Because I do not want to write this paper. And I've never told anybody this, but I sort of have this crush on Claire Bailey. Ever since sixth-grade social studies. She's not hot, exactly. Nobody'd say she was hot. I just like watching her. I like listening to her talk.

Claire leans forward in her desk now. "My parents and I talked about this last night at dinner, and they both said, both my mom and my dad said, that they don't think many people have one big defining moment in their lives. My dad said it would be impossible for him to pick just one big defining moment."

Mrs. Perris leans back with her hands around her right knee. She's grinning. You can tell she loves this. You can tell that she would pay to have Claire Bailey in her class. "What do the rest of you think about this?" she asks.

The rest of us just sit there. I know I'm thinking this sounds pretty good. I'm thinking, way to go, Claire.

Claire puts her hand up, like someone else is going to jump in here, and she says, "My mom said that for most people, their lives are just lots of little things, lots of day-to-day things that slowly add up. She said it would be an unusual person who could pick just one important moment."

Mrs. Perris nods, and Mrs. Perris says she agrees with Claire, that Claire has brought up some very good points. She looks around the room and says, "What do the rest of you think?" again. No one says anything. You can tell no one wants to wreck this. Maybe Claire's gotten us out of it.

But then Mrs. Perris sighs. And she checks the clock. Always a bad sign. "Well," she says, "why don't we say that you ask an adult to pick one important moment, one turning point?" She looks at Claire, and Claire shrugs. And we end up having to do the assignment anyway.

The day before the paper's due, I call up Aunt Jean and ask her. And she tells me some lame story about the one and only time she used marijuana, and how she'd thought she was going to die, and she never used drugs again. I have a feeling she's making it all up, that she thinks it's something she should tell me. I thank her, anyway, and I do get a page out of it. My margins are like an inch and a half.

Mrs. Perris gives me a C.

chapter six

AND CLAIRE—I COULDN'T believe this. I couldn't believe that maybe my luck was shifting—Claire showed up in my English class. She smiled at me and gave me a little wave and plunked down in a desk right at the front. First question out of Mr. Gott's mouth, Claire's hand was up, and she was saying something about how maybe Iago was just another side of Othello's character. And it was the eighth grade all over again. The teacher sitting on the desk, smiling. Claire leaning forward, shoving her hair up and out of the way. The rest of us sitting and staring.

Except this guy by the door, this punker with tattoos and a nose ring, put up his hand and said, "Wow. That's a really good point."

And I kicked myself. Because even if I hadn't read the

stupid play, I could have said that. I could have had Claire swivel around and give me that smart-ass grin.

That night, while Max was cruising around my bedroom, looking for stuff to chew on, I actually got the play out and tried to read it. I didn't get too far.

After school on Friday, I had a meeting with Mrs. Harriman. In any normal school they'd call her my counselor, but here, she was my mentor.

She came around her desk, smiling. "Hey there, Sam! And Max!" She waggled her fingers at him, and he wiggled in my arms and grinned and drooled simultaneously. Mrs. Harriman pointed to a baby swing in the corner. "Will he still sit in this? We shouldn't be long."

"Sure. He loves these things." I set him into the seat and dropped three or four Cheerios on the tray. "Any more than that and he throws them around," I said. I wanted her to know that I knew what I was doing. I set the swing in motion.

Mrs. Harriman went back around the desk and sat down. I sat in the chair across from her. We both watched Max carefully pick up one Cheerio and put it into his mouth. It took him about half an hour. He knew we were watching, so he gave us his "aren't I cute?" grin.

"Isn't he cute?" Mrs. Harriman said.

Actually, I thought he was freaking amazing. It seemed like just a few months ago he'd been lying around on his back, hitting himself in the eye with his own fist. Now he could pick up one Cheerio. It just knocked me out. I couldn't figure out how it happened. How all of a sudden he could do this stuff. One minute he's smearing juice and crackers in his hair, and the next minute he's almost like a real person.

"He looks just like you," Mrs. Harriman said.

"That's what people say." Although I couldn't see it. I thought he looked like Brittany—the round face and the blue eyes and the blonde hair.

"Okay." Mrs. Harriman straightened the papers on her desk, and I straightened up in my chair. So much for the touchy-feely crap. Talking to Mrs. Harriman, I always felt like I was about to take a test I hadn't studied for. A test I hadn't even known about.

She gave me her big smile. She had a big mouth, like what's her name, the actress, only not so pretty. "Your teachers are pleased, for the most part, Sam."

For the most part.

She tapped a long fingernail against a name. "Mr. Gott

says you've got a late paper in English?" She looked up at me, concerned, the smile fading, just a little.

One of the hardest things to get used to was the way they all talked about you to each other. All the time. Back at the regular school, none of my teachers knew what other classes I was taking or how I was doing in them. They didn't know anything. Here I felt like everybody knew everything there was to know about me. "I'm working on it," I said. "I just . . . " I shrugged. I hadn't even read the stupid short story. Every time I tried to read it, I fell asleep. And now we were already on *Othello* . . .

"Well, you'd better talk to him about it. I'm sure you and Mr. Gott can work something out. Okay?" Smile back, full width.

"Okay," I said.

She glanced back down at her papers. "You don't have a job, do you, Sam?"

"Uh . . . no." And, right away, that seemed like another wrong answer. I was starting to sweat, just a little. "See, the only job I could get after school, I couldn't make enough to pay for the day care . . . " Another thing Sam hadn't figured out. Another screwup.

Mrs. Harriman nodded. Smiling. Not so big. "And you're still living with your dad?"

"Yeah. Until I graduate. That's our deal." The Deal. "He'll pay the bills until I get my diploma. Then I'm going to work for Lawson Construction. On Highway 99? Dad knows Mr. Lawson. And I'll pay him back. For everything. The hospital bills and everything. I'll pay Dad. Not Mr. Lawson." Maybe if I just kept talking, I'd stumble on the answer she wanted. The right answer.

Max had finished the Cheerios. He banged his hand down, hard, on the tray, and shrieked.

Mrs. Harriman reached out and jiggled the swing. "Just a few more minutes, Max." He made a rude bubbly noise at her.

I gave him some more Cheerios.

Mrs. Harriman sat back in her chair. "And the parenting's going all right?"

"Going great."

I got asked this question at least once a week, by Mrs. McPherson, by the secretary, by Angie the aide. "How's it going, Sam? Going okay, Sam?" I wondered if they asked Gemma or Meredith or Christy. Jeez. Christy was a total ditz. Was it just because I was the only guy in the program? Or was it me? I looked at Max. "Everybody says he's doing fine."

"Absolutely. There's no question Max is thriving. There's no question he's getting lots of love." She leaned forward a little farther, peering up into my face. "It's you I'm worried about here, Sam. How are you doing?"

The way she said it, it sounded like a trick question. I smiled. "I'm doing fine, Mrs. Harriman."

She nodded. Smiled. Leaned back. "Have you thought about taking the SATs, Sam?"

"What?" I said. *This* was a trick question. "The what?"

"The SATs. They're the college . . ."

"I know what they are."

"Your PSATs last year were excellent, Sam. Believe me, I don't often see . . . your math score especially."

My PSAT scores. Somebody else had taken that test, gotten those scores. Somebody I'd heard about some-where. "I'm not going to college, Mrs. Harriman. That's not the deal. My dad and I . . . we've got this figured out. I'll work construction." I'll take responsibility.

"I understand that, Sam. But part of my job is to make sure you're aware of your options. Is working construction what you want to do?"

I laughed. I couldn't help it. Like I had options. Like any of this was what I wanted to do. Like I'd always dreamed of being a dad at seventeen. And the funny thing was, I had known what I wanted to do. I'd known exactly what I wanted to do. I'd taken a computer class, freshman year, and I'd loved it. I'd been good at it. It was like, yes, Sam Pettigrew, here's what you can do. Here's what you were meant to do. I was going to go to college. Major in engineering. Work with computers. Andy used to kid me about it. Computer Man Sam, and I knew he was jealous. But that Sam was somebody I'd maybe heard about some-where, too. "You can make good money in construction."

She tapped the papers. "I could talk to your father."

"No. Really." I took a deep breath. There had to be something I could say, some answer I could give that would make her drop this, that would make her let me out of here.

Max shrieked and banged the tray again. I stood up. "He wants out of this thing," I said. I unfastened him from the swing and picked him up.

"Several other students are taking the test." Mrs. Harriman was talking fast, before I could leave. "Some in the regular program, but in the parenting . . ." She checked her paper. "Angela Rodriguez. She has a toddler. And Gemma Moore. Brianna, Meredith, and the new mom . . ." She checked another paper. "Claire Bailey?"

I stood there, holding Max suspended in midair.

"I have some books," Mrs. Harriman said, "I thought maybe some of you . . . although I know how busy you are . . . but maybe you could find some time to study together. Support each other. We could work out some child care, I think."

Study together. "How often?" I asked.

Mrs. Harriman frowned. "What?"

"This study thing? How often?"

"Oh. Well. I suppose it depends. But the test is at the end of October. It would be great if you could meet once or even twice a week."

And I knew she was thinking, twice a week, that's a lot. And I was thinking, twice a week with Claire. Not enough. I nodded. Max kicked his legs against my stomach.

"I just think, Sam," Mrs. Harriman said, "it's one thing you could do for yourself. Taking this test. Keeping a door open."

I sat back down, Max heavy on my lap. "Okay," I said. "What do I have to do?"

chapter seven

IT COST TWENTY-FOUR bucks to take the SATs. Which, of course, I didn't have. So I borrowed it from Aunt Jean. I had to tell her what it was for, so she could write the check. "I'll pay it back," I said. And I waited for her to say something. Something like "Are you out of your mind?" But she just rocked Max on her hip and smiled and said, "Sure, Sam. No problem."

That night, at home again, I sat there in my room, looking at Aunt Jean's check, and I started to wonder if maybe I was going crazy. Not just taking the SATs— which was pretty nuts—but the way I'd started thinking about Claire. The way I was thinking about Claire all the time.

I'd open the government book, and I'd start wondering

what Claire was studying. Giving Max a bottle, I'd think about Claire feeding Emily. Driving to school, doing laundry, changing diapers. We were late to school twice because I couldn't get my hair to lie down right. I'd even dug out an old tube of Clearasil and tried to hide the zit on my chin.

What was crazy was I had not thought about a girl, any girl, like this, since Brittany told me she was pregnant.

Mrs. Harriman stopped me in the hall on Wednesday. "Okay, Sam. I've worked out an after-school schedule for you guys. There'll only be three of you. Most of the girls can't make it." I held my breath. "You and Gemma and Claire . . ." I let my breath out. ". . . will meet starting Monday. 2:30 in the library." She looked at me. "You need to write this down in your planner, Sam."

"I'll remember."

I wondered if Mrs. Harriman suspected why I was doing this. And, if she knew, if they knew Sam Pettigrew was maybe certifiably nuts, would they let me keep Max? Are crazy people allowed to be parents?

And then I started thinking about how much I really needed a haircut.

On Monday, Max and I were late. For some reason, he had slept in until 7:00, and our whole morning thing was wrecked. I barely got a chance to shower, and I nicked myself about fifteen times shaving.

I spent the whole day waiting for 2:30 and trying not to mess with my hair.

Even though I ran all the way from Ms. Garcia's classroom, Claire and Gemma were already in the library when I got there, sitting at the round table in the corner. Claire grabbed my hand as I sat down, which pretty much knocked the wind out of me. "Tell me that Emily's okay," she said.

"What?" My voice was a croak.

"Emily's fine," Gemma said. "Martine Vickers is looking after all three kids. She has like ten little brothers and sisters. Believe me, she knows what she's doing." Gemma was wearing a T-shirt that said "What would Buddha do?" in big letters.

I gently pulled my hand out from under Claire's and managed to connect my lungs back to my brain. "Martine's in my government class. She's okay." Yesterday, Mr. Walker had asked which party the president belonged to, and Martine had said, seriously,

"Communist?" I decided Claire didn't need to know that.

Claire was shaking her head. "But *three* babies?"

"Max is probably asleep," I said. Of course he was. He was sleeping now so he could keep me up tonight.

"They'll be fine." Gemma started unloading a huge pile of books out of her backpack. "Okay. Mrs. Harriman gave me these to help us study. Let's get to work."

And we did, which sort of surprised me. Gemma had a whole schedule worked out, and we spent the next hour doing practice math problems and vocabulary tests and word analogies. "Just to see where we stand," Gemma said. I did okay on all the math stuff, but Claire and Gemma were way better than me at the verbal.

Gemma shook her head at my analogies worksheet. "English *is* your native tongue?"

"Ha-ha. Very funny."

Claire leaned over to look, too. "You took the PSATs, right?"

"Right."

"And what was your verbal score?" She and Gemma were both grinning.

"It was above the average," I said.

They laughed. "Well," Gemma said, tapping the page

with one of her long purple fingernails. "You're going to have to do better than this if you want to get into college."

I leaned back in my chair. I was a little pissed. "Are you really going to college, Gemma?"

She frowned at me. "You bet I am, sucker. My husband, Michael? He has a good job, and he's up for a raise in six months. Plus they have on-site day care. My mom is helping us out. And once I'm done and working, Michael's going to college, too."

She made it all sound like a fact, like a done deal. She made it sound like she had everything under control. Like Kristin never decided to sleep in for an extra hour and ruin the whole morning.

Claire was leaning back in her chair. She looked a little like the rest of us had looked in English, when she started in on Othello and What's-His-Name.

"Plus . . . " There was no stopping Gemma once she got going. "I'm the perfect scholarship candidate. I'm a low-income African-American female with good grades and great math scores. I want to major in chemical engineering. It's true, I'm a teenage mother, but I'm enrolled in this school to learn to be a better parent." She shrugged. "I've overcome more adversity than those white admissions officers have ever dreamed of." She looked at her watch. "Oh. Hey. I've got to try to catch Mr. Walker before he leaves." She pointed at the worksheets. "Why don't you guys do some more analogies."

Claire and I watched her lope off and out the door. Claire looked at me. "You believe all that? That she's going to make all that work?"

I shook my head. "I don't know. Gemma's got it pretty together." Actually, I liked Gemma. She was easier to talk to than most of the other moms. And Michael always said hi to me when he came to pick up her and Kristin. "Michael's a nice guy." I thought about it. "He's older than us, I think."

Claire picked up her hair and held it off the back of her neck. "It probably makes a big difference. When there's two of you."

At last. I had been trying to figure out how to work around to asking. I picked up a pencil, then put it down again. "So you're not living with Emily's father?"

"Trent?" Claire laughed. She dropped her hair, and it fell in this dark slow cloud back around her shoulders. "No. We're not living with Trent."

"Trent . . . ?" I was wracking my brain. There were a couple of Trents at Willamette View.

Claire started rolling up the corner of one of the worksheets. "You don't know him. He goes to Hillsboro."

"So how'd you meet him?" I relaxed back in my chair a little.

She looked at me, quick, out of the corner of her eyes. "You're going to laugh." She was smiling a little.

I started to smile, too. "Try me."

She was rolling the whole worksheet up now. "I met him at a debate competition."

She was right. I did laugh, once, loud enough to get a look from Ms. Lucchesi behind her desk. I leaned forward and lowered my voice. "A debate competition?"

"They're more romantic than you'd think. You know. All that . . . "

"Arguing," I said, and she laughed and hit me, lightly, with the rolled up paper.

"So . . . " I picked up a worksheet and started rolling it. "Do you see him? Trent?"

She sighed. "He pays child support. And we have this

visitation deal. He can take Emily on weekends. Only he hasn't shown up the last two." She rolled her eyes. "Becky? She has a four-month-old? She used to go to Hillsboro, and she said she heard he's dating some freshman."

I felt something loosen in my chest. "What a jerk," I said. And I was thinking, "Way to go, Trent."

"What about you?" she said. "Are you living with Brittany?"

I unrolled the worksheet.

"That's Max's mom, right? Brittany Ames?"

"How did you know that?"

"You guys were hot news there for a while, Sam." She shrugged. "You know high school."

"Yeah. Well. Brittany and her parents moved to Boise. I send them pictures and stuff." I smoothed the worksheet, carefully. "Brittany sort of couldn't do the mothering thing." And I thought about Brittany, and how it must have been for her. How hard to decide to give him up. How it hadn't made sense to me at the time.

Claire was nodding. "I can respect that. I mean, before I decided to keep Emily, I did research. I considered all my options."

I laughed. "I'll bet you did."

She leaned forward and shoved her hair back from her face. "But I think it's amazing what you're doing, Sam. How you're being such a great dad."

My face flushed hot and red. I wanted to say I wasn't great. But I knew it would sound whiny and lame.

"Are you guys living at home?" Claire asked.

I nodded. "Yeah. With my dad."

"I live with my mom and my dad and my little sister," Claire said. "And they all, let me tell you, just love Emily to bits." She flicked a No. Two pencil, and it spun off the table and onto the floor. "I cannot wait to get out and have a place of our own."

I nodded.

"Although . . . " She waved her hand at the papers and books. "I mean. I want to go to college. It's the best thing for me and for Emily. And I'll have to live at home to do that."

I nodded again.

She sighed. "When I decided to keep Emily, my parents kept saying, 'Think, Claire. This is the rest of your life.' And I kept saying, 'Yes, that's why I know I have to do this.'" She looked at me, her eyes bright and intense.

"You know what I mean? Didn't you just know what you wanted to do?"

I'd known what I *had* to do. "I know what you mean," I said.

She smiled at me. "I was so glad to see you there in the hall that day, Sam. I felt so . . . relieved."

"Yeah," I said. "Me too." And I thought how weird this was. How weird it was that Claire Bailey and I finally had something in common.

MARGARET BECHARD

chapter **eight**

"HOW DID THIS HAPPEN?" Andy says to me.

We're leaning against the gym wall, watching a substitute teacher try to get our PE class to play dodgeball.

"Friday night. After Melissa's party."

"What about the big fight?" He's shaking his head, not totally believing this.

"We made up," I say, and I can't stop grinning. Although now, here in the hot smelly gym, I'm wondering if it did really happen. Maybe it was just one of my more vivid fantasies.

Larissa Hulce is telling the substitute that we're not allowed to play dodgeball anymore because some kid got hurt last year, and the parents complained. And then somebody else says we *can* play dodgeball, only we have to call it "catch and throw." The substitute's eyes are starting to roll up into his head.

"I think he's having a seizure," Andy says. He starts to push off the wall, grinning, ready to get into this.

"Naw, he's just trying to check the clock." I'm afraid Andy's going to get distracted, start torturing substitutes, stop talking to me. "Where were you and Jenny, anyway?" I ask, quickly.

"Jenny's car wouldn't start. We got there late." He swivels his head to look at me. "At your house, huh?" he says.

I nod. I'm starting to feel little shots of guilt. Because I know that's what girls think. That they have sex with some guy and immediately he tells all his friends. But I've only told Andy. And it's not because I'm bragging. It's just that talking about it makes it seems like it really happened.

I'm feeling nervous, too. I haven't seen Brittany or talked to her since that night. I called on Saturday, and again on Sunday, but her mother answered both times. I was afraid—I don't know—it seemed like Mrs. Ames might be able to tell, just from hearing my voice—I'd hung up without saying anything.

I'm wondering what Brittany is thinking. I'm wondering if she's regretting it.

I'm wondering if she'll want to do it again.

I don't see her until third period. Chemistry. She's sitting in the back of the room. I walk in the door, and it's like one of those retarded music videos that I hate. All of a sudden, the space from the door, where I am, to the back of the room, where Brittany is sitting with two of her friends, all of a sudden it stretches out in front of me, on and on for miles. There's no point in even trying to walk so far.

And if I did get there, what would I say to her?

So I stand there in the doorway, kids bumping into me and swearing. "Jeez, Sam. What's your problem? You coming or going, Sam?"

And it gets to be enough—I mean, we're making enough of a commotion—that Brittany looks up and sees me. I want to just turn around. Just turn around, leave, go home, move to another town, another state.

But I can't. There are kids piled up behind me.

Then Brittany says, "Sam!" And, saying my name, she changes everything back to normal. She gets up and crosses the room. It's not so far at all. A few feet. Really, that's it. And she puts her arms around me and she kisses me, right there in the doorway to chemistry.

"Oh, great," Megan Armstrong says. "Now we'll never get in the room."

It turns out, Brittany does want to have sex again.

Once at a party, in a back bedroom, kids talking outside, laughing.

Once in my car, with the radio playing and me worrying about the battery.

Mostly at Brittany's house. After school. In her room. She has a great room, about twice the size of mine. She has a big bed and a couch. A TV and a VCR and a CD player. Her own bathroom. If you just had a refrigerator, you could live in there. You'd never have to leave. I say that to her, and she laughs, leaning over me, her hand on my arm, her long blonde hair tickling against my chest. And she says, "You're a funny guy, Sam. You say the funniest things."

The fifth time, we're at my house. "Weezer" on the CD player again. I'm lying in bed, afterward, watching her get dressed. She's putting on her bra. Bras make a lot more sense when you can see them, although she does this thing, fastens it in front, and then twists it around so the fastener's in the back. I've never seen anybody in a movie do that, and it's fun to watch. Like watching a magician or something. Houdini.

And I just kind of blurt it out. I say, "Was it okay?"

She turns around and looks at me, backlit by the window. I can't see her face. She's wearing just her bra and underwear, these little pink underwear things with butterflies on the sides. "What?" she asks.

I roll over onto my back. I once saw this TV show where somebody said, "If you're doing it, you should be able to talk about it." Only, now that we are doing it, it seems almost impossible to talk about. I can't even figure out what to call it. Screwing? Making love? "Did you have a good time?"

She doesn't say anything. I know she's just standing there. A new track starts on the CD. And then she says, "Oh. Oh, yeah. It was great."

Then, maybe she realizes . . . maybe she knows it's been like a few seconds too long. Because she comes over and kneels on the edge of the bed, and I sit up, and she hugs me. "Really," she says.

I don't know if she's just saying it because she thinks she's supposed to say it. Or because she thinks I want her to say it. Or is she saying she likes it because she's sup-posed to like it? Or does she really like it?

Thinking about it is just as bad as talking about it. So I hug her back. And I say, "Good. That's good. I'm glad."

Because, for me, no question. I like it a lot. I think sex is great.

But I like Brittany a lot, too.

I like being with her. Just sitting next to her in a movie. Or holding hands in the hall at school. We go to the mall, and I like just walking around with her, talking to her about the people we see and the stuff for sale. She's funny and she's nice. And she's going out with me.

Andy and I are talking one day, in the library. We're supposed to be researching South Africa, but Andy's clicking around, checking out Web sites. He finds this one called "The Daily Bikini," which pretty much describes it. And I don't know what I say, I say some-thing like, "I don't think she looks as good as Brittany." And Andy laughs so hard, he nearly falls off his chair. "Man," he says, finally, shaking his head. "Man, you've got it bad."

And I laugh, too. Because it's true.

I don't tell Andy, but I'm working on this idea. What

I would really like to do, what I've been thinking about for a long time, is I'd like to just spend a whole night with Brittany. Like in those movies. Not the sex part, so much. The part afterward. I want to fall asleep and wake up and find her asleep with her head on my chest. I want to fall asleep and wake up and just find her there with me.

Then, early in April, Dad tells me he's going the next weekend to a friend's cabin up on Hood. Fishing for chinook. He says I can come along, but I say, "I've got a lot of homework," and he drops it.

The Saturday before, at the movies, I ask Brittany, like it doesn't matter, if she's going anywhere next weekend. And she says no, where would she go?

I'm starting to work it all out. How Brittany can tell her parents she's staying at Megan's Saturday night. How I'll get a lot of candles, put them around my room. Maybe some wine, if Andy's sister is in a good mood. How we can have breakfast in the morning. We could have Lucky Charms or Sugar Pops. Something goofy, to make her laugh. I have it all worked out.

That Tuesday, she tells me she's pregnant.

chapter nine

MONDAYS AND WEDNESDAYS WERE now my favorite days of the week. No question. I tried to make sure I had clean clothes, and I spent as much extra time as I could shaving and trying to get my hair to lie down. Then I'd wait for 2:30. "The SAT group," Claire called it. As if it were a club or something. As if it were important to her, too.

School started going faster. Suddenly, it was the first Wednesday in October. We only had four more times to meet, and I was getting bummed out. What would happen after we took the test? Would I still see Claire?

For some reason, Max fell asleep halfway through lunch that day. Just put his head down on the tray of the high chair and conked out, right in the middle of the

MARGARET BECHARD

noisy cafeteria. I finished my burger and carried him back to the day care.

Tawna and Nicole were already in the crawler room. Tawna was in the rocking chair, nursing Kylie, a blanket thrown over her so you could hardly tell what was going on. Nicole was trying to make a bottle, with Augusto hanging onto her leg and screaming.

I put Max, still zonked, in one of the swings. I waited for them to tell me what I'd done wrong, but Nicole just said, "Hey, Sam. How's it going?" Augusto screamed louder.

He was going to wake up Max. "Dude," I said. "What's the problem?" I went over and pried his fingers off her pants leg and picked him up. He stopped crying and leaned back in my arms, staring at me very seriously.

"What's going on with you and Gemma in the afternoons, Sam?" Tawna asked. She adjusted Kylie under the blanket.

I kept looking at Augusto. "It's this study thing. The SAT group," I added.

"Oh, yeah," Nicole said. She'd finished filling the bottle with milk. "Mrs. Harriman talked to me about that, too. But there's just no way. I have to be at work at

3:00." She put the bottle in the microwave. Augusto leaned toward it, watching the bottle go around.

"At least I don't have to worry about that," Tawna said. "I'm going into the Army when I graduate."

Nicole and I both turned and looked at her. "The Army?" I said. "No kidding?"

"Yeah. Garrett's mom is going to look after Kylie." Tawna's face crumpled a little. "I'll miss her so much."

"It'll be good," Nicole said. "For all of you." She nudged me sharply.

"Sure. It'll be great."

The microwave dinged, and Augusto gave a little excited yip. I put him in his swing, and Nicole handed him the bottle. "What are you going to do after you graduate?" I asked Nicole.

"There's an early childhood education program at the community college. I can do a lot of it nights, when Jorge can baby-sit." Nicole glanced at me. "I'd like to work with little kids, you know. Kind of like this. Like Mrs. McPherson does."

I nodded. "I can see you doing that. I can see you being good at it."

She grinned and bent down to wrap a blanket around

Augusto. He was sucking hard on the bottle, his eyes already half-closed. "I've almost gotten him to give up the bottle at home," Nicole said. She looked over at Max, slumped in the swing, his head back, his mouth open. "Max drinks out of a cup, doesn't he?"

"Oh, yeah." Max hated the cup I'd bought. He threw it on the floor every time I gave it to him.

"You don't want them to get too dependent on the bottle," Nicole said, like she knew I was lying.

"Right," I said. And I had a picture of Max. Sixteen years old, hanging out with his friends, still drinking out of his bottle. We'd try the cup again tonight.

Tawna unplugged Kylie and stood up. "What about you, Sam? What are you going to do after you graduate?"

I was still on the bottle thing, and it took me a second. "What? Oh. Construction, I guess."

Tawna frowned at me. "So why are you taking the SAT's?"

The door opened, and Claire came in. She had Emily draped over her shoulder. She smiled at Tawna and Nicole, then turned to me. "Sam, Gemma's got a doctor's appointment, so she can't make it to the SAT group today."

"Hey," I said. "Hey. That's too bad." But my brain was shouting, *No Gemma! Yes!*

"So, I was thinking," Claire said, "maybe we should just go over to my house. Where we'd be more comfortable."

"Your house?" My voice went up a little. I saw Nicole give Tawna a look, and I wished Claire and I were not having this conversation here. I coughed. "We can meet at your house?"

"Yeah. It's not far. Just over on Conestoga."

The last time I had gone over to a girl's house, I had gone to Brittany's. And we hadn't exactly studied.

"I know what you're thinking," Claire said, "but don't worry about it. We'll get a lot done. My sister will be there to look after the babies."

Max. I hadn't even thought about Max. And why couldn't I go over to somebody's house after school like a normal person. "Okay," I said. "Sure. Let's study at your house."

After school, Max and I followed Claire's orange VW van over to her house. I unloaded Max and the diaper bag and my backpack and met Claire at the front door. Emily was crying. Loudly. "Come on in," Claire said.

It was the kind of house where you walk straight into the living room. And the living room was crammed with baby stuff—a swing, a jumper chair, a cradle, a blanket covered in rattles and stuffed animals.

"Whoa," I said. Max was wiggling in my arms, trying to get down. He'd spotted the plastic slide in the corner. Baby heaven.

"I know," Claire said. "Crazy, isn't it?" She put Emily down on the couch. Emily screamed louder. "My mom and my grandmother go to garage sales every weekend."

Max had wiggled down so far in my arms, I was holding him by the armpits. "Is it okay if he plays with this stuff?"

"Sure. Put him anywhere." Claire shrugged out of her jacket and started pulling off Emily's sweater and hat.

I set Max down next to the slide. He pulled himself up on his feet, holding onto the sides. At home, he had the high chair in the kitchen and the crib in my bedroom. I used his car seat for a baby chair. "Your dad doesn't mind all . . . all this?" I said.

"My dad loves Emily more than me and my sister."

I looked at her, but she was smiling. She sat down, with Emily in her lap, and started reaching under her shirt. I caught just a flash of white, a flash of her breast. "I really, really have to feed her," Claire said.

"Right," I said. "Sure. No problem." I turned around and pulled off Max's sweatshirt. Then I helped him climb up the steps of the slide.

In ninth grade, I would have paid fifty bucks to see Claire Bailey's breasts.

I helped Max slide down. He landed on the floor with a bump, but he just rolled over and crawled back to the steps.

At least Emily had stopped screaming. "This doesn't bother you, does it?" Claire asked.

I glanced back, quick. She'd covered Emily and everything else with a blanket. I turned around. "I've seen it before."

She grinned. "I bet you've seen a lot. I bet you've heard a lot."

"You wouldn't believe it."

"You know," Claire said, "I've always meant to apologize. For that first day. I acted like such a . . ." She laughed. "Such a baby."

"It was okay. I didn't mind." I helped Max back to the steps.

"Because now, I mean, I'm so much more relaxed and in control. I can't believe how natural it all feels."

I nodded and tried to look like I had any idea what she was talking about. "You look pretty natural," I said.

She smiled at me like I'd just given her some great compliment. Said she was beautiful or something.

And, just for a few seconds—and this was completely crazy—this was nuts—I mean, she was breastfeeding, Max was climbing up the slide—don't be stupid, Sam. But, for a few seconds, I thought, maybe we will be here alone. Claire's smile widened, and her eyes got bigger. Maybe she'd made up the whole thing about her sister coming home.

And maybe this was all in my head. Just because I was crazy didn't mean Claire was.

The front door banged open. A girl about thirteen rushed in. She had long dark hair, like Claire's, but hers was pulled back in a single fat braid. "I'm home!" she shouted at the top of her lungs.

"Jeez, Natalie," Claire said.

Natalie dumped a huge backpack next to the door. She spotted Max. "Ooh. Another baby!"

Max grinned, showing off his teeth and his drool. He

pulled himself up onto his feet. "Wow-wow," he said.

"Omigod! He talks! What's his name?" Natalie wove her way through the baby stuff to us.

"His name's Max," I said. Natalie hadn't looked at me yet, and she didn't now.

"Max," she said. She sat down and held out her hand, like you would to a strange dog. "Hi, Max. Maxie, Max-Max. How old is he?"

"Almost eleven months."

"Does he walk yet?"

"No."

As if to prove I was wrong, Max let go of the slide and took two wobbly steps toward Natalie.

"Oh," she said. "He'll be walking really soon. You can tell."

Even a kid knew more about it than I did.

"Don't mind her, Sam," Claire said. "Natalie's a little obsessed with babies."

"I'm going to be a pediatrician," Natalie said, picking Max up.

"Look, Nat. We need you to baby-sit, okay? While we study?"

"Okay," Natalie said.

Claire looked at me. "There's Coke in the fridge, Sam. I thought we could work in the kitchen. As soon as I'm done here."

"Sure." All of a sudden, I felt like I was one more thing cluttering up the room.

There was more baby stuff in the kitchen. A high chair, another swing, another bouncy baby seat. It was like Emily was triplets or quadruplets.

I grabbed a Coke. I was trying to be glad that Natalie had really showed up. And I was wondering if Claire was glad, when the back door opened and a woman with curly gray hair, dressed in a black suit, walked in.

I jumped about a foot and a half.

"That should hold her for a little bit." Claire walked in from the living room, tucking her shirt into her jeans. She stopped in the doorway. "Mom!"

"Well." Mrs. Bailey's eyebrows went up exactly like Claire's. "What's going on?"

Nothing. Nothing's going on, I thought. But I couldn't say it.

"This is Sam Pettigrew," Claire said. "We're studying for the SATs, Mom. Remember? You thought it was such a great idea?"

"Yes, Claire, I remember," Mrs. Bailey said. "But why are you *here*?"

"Because Gemma couldn't come today, and it was just easier and more comfortable to come over here." Claire sounded like she was explaining to a two-year-old. "Why are you here now?"

Mrs. Bailey rubbed at her forehead. "A client canceled. What about Emily? Have you fed her?"

"Yes, of course."

"And you put her on her back? You know . . ."

"Mom. I abandoned her in the middle of the freeway. What do you think? Natalie's got her."

"Okay. Okay." Mrs. Bailey glanced at me, then away. "You know, I did an Internet search, and I found some interesting Web sites. Some good information on solid food . . ."

"Mom."

"She'd sleep better at night . . ."

"Mom." Claire's voice was going up on each successive *mom*.

Mrs. Bailey spread out her hands. "Okay. Okay," she said again. "I'll go help Natalie." She gave me a smile. "It was nice to meet you, Adam."

"Sam," I said.

She nodded. "Well. You two get to work, then." And she went out of the room.

"Ooh." Claire shuddered all over. "Ooh. She treats me like a total idiot."

But I was standing there, thinking how great it would be. To have someone searching the Internet. Someone else who knew to put them on their backs. "Yeah," I said. "I can see how it would drive you nuts."

Claire and I did word analogies for half an hour. Then I made up an excuse about Dad needing me, and Max and I went home.

chapter **ten**

To take the SATs, I had to be at Willamette View at 8:00 in the morning. I told Dad I had a thing at school. A community service thing.

I dropped Max off with Aunt Jean at 7:15. At Aunt Jean and Uncle Ted's, you always went through the back door, straight into their kitchen. I don't know if the front door even opened. Aunt Jean was waiting at the kitchen table, dressed in jeans and a sweater, reading the paper. She and Uncle Ted had already had breakfast. Clean dishes were draining by the sink. She'd probably mopped all the floors and cleaned the bathrooms, too.

She held out her hands to Max. "Come here, pumpkin." Max leaned out of my arms toward her, giving her his big old wet Max grin. She hugged him close and

MARGARET BECHARD

smiled at me. "I think he remembers me, don't you?"

"Oh, definitely," I said. I didn't tell her that Max did that to everybody. I didn't tell her that Max would jump into the arms of a drooling, greasy, Hell's Angel biker.

I put the diaper bag on the table. "There's diapers and extra clothes. And cereal and fruit for his lunch. And I put in two bottles and some extra formula." I ran my hand through my hair, going over the list in my head. "And Cheerios. I didn't know if you'd have Cheerios."

Aunt Jean nodded and smiled and pressed her face against Max's head. She was swaying him back and forth, and he had relaxed his body into hers.

"I'll leave you the car seat, too. In case you want to go somewhere." I set it down on the floor. All of a sudden, without the car seat or the diaper bag or Max, my hands felt light and empty. I jammed them into my pockets. "I should be home by noon, but I'm not sure . . ."

Aunt Jean stopped swaying. She put one hand on my arm and looked up into my face. "You take just as long as you need, Sam. You don't rush because you're worried about us."

I realized that Uncle Ted was standing in the doorway to the living room. "Well," I said. "I appreciate this.

Thanks a lot." And I lifted my chin, so he'd know I was talking to him, too.

He smiled and waved a hand. "No problem, Sam."

There was, sort of, this family joke. That Uncle Ted was only allowed to say twenty words in any given year. And he'd just used three up on me.

Aunt Jean squeezed my arm. "You just think about that test," she said. Then, more softly, "You know, your mom always wanted you to go to college, Sam."

"Okay," I said. "Okay." I smiled down at her, and then I took off, quick.

The wind was blowing hard and cold when I pulled into the lot at Willamette View. I sat in the car for a minute, watching the ropes bang and rattle on the flag-pole. Thinking about how stupid this was. Thinking how nice it would be to lean the seat back and spend the next four hours sleeping. Thinking about Aunt Jean holding Max, and Uncle Ted standing in the doorway, smiling. How happy Max had looked.

I climbed out of the car and let the wind push me across the parking lot to the doors of the school.

I hadn't been inside this place in a long time. I'd for-gotten all the big windows and the light. The vending machines against the walls. The latte stand, closed today. And the posters, all over the place, advertising dances and games and club meetings.

There were kids standing in a long line, waiting to check in. I knew most of them didn't go to this school. They were just here to take the test. Like me. But a lot of them were from Willamette View, and I recognized some of them.

I couldn't see Gemma or Claire anywhere.

The door banged against my heel. "Move your butt, buddy." A girl with bleached white hair and a tongue stud pushed past me.

I followed her over to the end of the line. When I got to the front, a happy-looking woman took my ticket and gave me my room assignment. "Room 23A. There are people in the halls to direct you," she said.

I'd had sophomore English in 23A. "I know where it is," I said.

I don't know what I'd been thinking, because I had taken the PSATs. But maybe because we'd been studying together. Maybe because it had been me and Claire and Gemma for the past weeks, I guess I'd been thinking it would be just us today, too. Off in some room by ourselves.

I walked into 23A. There were already kids there. Including Andy.

Andy saw me, and for a second, he looked surprised. Shocked. But then he grinned and pointed to the desk behind him.

I went over and sat down. "Andy. How's it goin'?" And I remembered I hadn't gone to his football game, hadn't called him back, hadn't wanted to call him back.

Andy turned in his desk. He'd buzzed off his hair, so all he had was black fuzz. It made him look older. And I wondered how I looked to him. "I didn't know you'd be here," he said.

I shrugged. "Yeah. Well." I dug out my calculator and my two No. Two pencils and lined them up on the desk.

At the front of the room, the monitor said, "We're going to get started, people. No more talking." And Andy turned back around.

The first part of the test was math, which was good. If I'd had to start out with the verbal crap, I would have just quit. But the math—it was nice to just spend some time working with numbers, feeling them sort of slide around and click together. I started remembering when math had been fun.

The math sort of pulled me through the verbal sections. Until the last one. I got totally bogged down in some long thing about women scientists in Florence. Or maybe it was a woman scientist named Florence. I couldn't figure out what was going on. I stared at the back of Andy's head, his neck white and clean against the dark line of his hair. And I thought about what Claire had said about college being good for Emily. And, just for a little while, I thought about me going to college. And how maybe, maybe I could somehow make it work out. For me and Max.

Andy and I walked out together when the test was over. Andy was moaning, softly, and shaking his head. "'Equalize:parity,'" he said. "Do you even know what that means? 'Parity?'"

"I think I left it blank," I said.

"Me, too." He shook his head. "And that last math section? They expect us to know this stuff?" He looked at me. "But I suppose you got them all right. Sam the math whiz." And then his face turned red, like he'd said something wrong.

But I laughed. Because it felt good to be walking down that hall again, talking to Andy, listening to Andy bitch. "The last section sucked," I said.

Andy looked happier. "It did! It totally and completely sucked!"

"Wait up, guys." Claire pushed her way through the crowd. "What'd you think? How'd you do? The word analogies?" She pointed at me.

I held out my hand and waggled it from side to side. "The geometry?"

She waggled her hand at me. We both laughed. I pointed at Andy. "You remember Andy?"

"Sure." Claire gave him a grin. "How's it going?"

Andy was looking from me to Claire and back at me. If he were in a cartoon, his eyes would be bugging out of his head, and his jaw would be on the floor. "Claire Bailey," he said, finally. Claire and I laughed again.

We walked out into the commons. "I'm parked by the flagpole," I said.

"Me, too," Claire said, and we grinned at each other. Like parking in the same place meant something.

Andy frowned. "I'm over by the gym."

"Well, I'll call you sometime then," I said.

"Okay," Andy said. And I knew he watched Claire and me as we walked out the doors.

We stopped out on the sidewalk. I didn't want to just

go get in my car, drive away. I wanted to hang onto this for a few minutes.

"What's wrong, Sam?" Claire asked. "You look funny."

"Just thinking about the test," I said.

She stepped closer to me, letting my body shield her from the wind. I could smell her perfume and just the faintest whiff of baby wipes. "I was thinking maybe we could go to Burger King. You know. To celebrate. Seeing as how we're baby-free."

I immediately thought of all the reasons I couldn't— I'd promised Dad I'd vacuum the living room and clean the bathrooms. There was laundry, homework. Max. Worst of all: I had exactly fifty-eight cents in my pocket.

"My dad gave me twenty bucks last night," Claire said. "My treat." She stepped closer and looked up at me smiling, smiling like she had at her house.

"Okay," I said. "I'll follow you over there."

"No. Come in my car. It'll be more fun."

As I climbed into the van's passenger seat, Claire said, "Do you see Andy a lot?"

I shook my head. "No. Hardly at all. Well. Never, in fact."

She started the engine. "I know. I never see my old

friends, either. It's like they thought pregnancy was contagious or something. Either that or I was from some CBS Afternoon Special." She made her voice high and goofy. "'Oh, Claire. What's it like?'"

"Poster child for the dangers of teenage sex," I said. And we both laughed. I fastened my seat belt. "Could we go to Taco Bell? Instead of Burger King?"

"Taco Bell?" Claire made a face.

"I haven't eaten at Taco Bell in a long, long time." And I'd missed Taco Bell.

Claire leaned over. She put her hand on my thigh. "Well, today's your lucky day, Sam Pettigrew. Taco Bell it is."

"Great," I said. Although now all I could think about was her hand on my leg, and how I'd missed that, too.

chapter eleven

WHEN MOM COMES HOME from the hospital, that last time, she brings the hospital bed with her. She jokes about that as she lies there in the living room. She lets me push the buttons, making the head and the foot go up and down. She laughs. Her face is as white as the sheets and pillowcases. I laugh, too, although I'm really sort of afraid of that bed. That bed and her white, white face.

I hear Aunt Jean talking on the phone to Aunt Connie. "She wants to die at home."

Fourth grade is not my best year in school. I have Mrs. D'Nunnzio. All the kids call her Dragon Breath. But, for the first time since September, I want to go to school in the morning. I get there early every day.

Aunt Jean is always waiting in the kitchen when I get home, and she always says, "Go in and talk to your mother. Tell her what you did today." I go in the living room, and Mom smiles and pats the bed beside her. I climb up, careful not to jostle her, careful not to make her scrunch up her face and gasp. "Start at the beginning," she says, and I do. "First," I say, "I walked to school." Sometimes I show her papers I'd worked on or pictures I'd drawn. When she gets tired, she closes her eyes, and she has lines on her eyelids, blue lines just like the ones on my notebook paper. After a few days, we don't push the buttons on the bed.

When Aunt Jean says, "You can't climb on the bed anymore, sweetie pie," I'm glad. And I feel bad that I'm glad.

That last morning, when I wake up, Aunt Jean and Dad are both in the living room. Dad is holding Mom's hand, looking down at her. I can hear her breathing, right across the room. I've never been able to hear her breathe like that before. It's loud and raspy, almost like the noise Dad makes when he snores.

"I'm going to be late for school," I say, loud, louder than those stuttery breaths.

MARGARET BECHARD

Aunt Jean and Dad both look at me. Dad says, "You know, Sam . . ." He looks at Aunt Jean, clears his throat. "You know, buddy, I think you can miss school today."

I shake my head. "No. I can't. We have a test today. A spelling test. I can't miss it."

Aunt Jean drives me to school.

There's a nurse there when I get home. She's standing by Mom, stroking her hair. Dad is still holding Mom's hand, only he's sitting on one of the chairs from the dining room, pushed up close to the bed. Mom's still taking those loud, loud breaths.

"Can she hear us?" Dad whispers. "Does she know we're here?"

"Theresa's in a deep coma, Mitch," the nurse says. She keeps stroking Mom's hair. "But I think she knows we're here."

I want to tell her to stop touching my mother. I want to tell her to get out of our house.

Suddenly, there's silence. The hoarse breaths stop. And even though I'm standing there, holding onto the door frame, I feel like I'm falling forward into the silence.

Mom gasps, sighs, and the breathing starts again.

"Not long now," the nurse whispers.

But it is long. All that afternoon and evening, no matter where I go in the house, I can hear her breathing. Or worse, not breathing. I go in Mom and Dad's bedroom, and I lie on Dad's side of the bed, and I watch a show on the Discovery Channel. A show about wolverines.

Dad comes in and asks if I want to come to the living room for a minute. I shake my head. And Aunt Jean comes in and asks if I need anything. I shake my head again.

Late that night, after Aunt Jean has gone to bed in the spare bedroom, I go in the living room. The only light is from the night light Dad put in next to the TV, so he could see to get around. My old night light that had been in the bathroom drawer ever since I got too old to need it.

Dad is asleep on the couch, one arm thrown over his face. The other one dangles on the floor. Like he just fell down there. Too tired to move. He doesn't fit on that couch.

I wait, making sure he's really asleep. And then I cross to the hospital bed, and I crawl underneath it. I lie on my back, staring up at the wires and the boxes, all the things that make the bed go up and down. And I start to count the breaths. "One, two, three," I whisper. I pause when she pauses, then start the count over again. "One, two, three." I make my own breaths come in time with my mother's.

When I wake up the next morning, I'm in my own bed. It's late. I can tell because the sun is all the way across my desk. The house is very, very quiet.

chapter twelve

MS. GARCIA STOPPED BY the iMac on Monday. She crouched down next to me, which made her so short she nearly disappeared under the table. "So how did the SATs go, Sam?" she whispered.

It took me a minute to remember. "The math was okay, I think," I said. When I'd gotten back to Aunt Jean's, Max had been crying, and she'd thought he had a fever. I ended up having to take him to the doctor, and he had an ear infection. We hadn't slept a lot Saturday or Sunday night.

Ms. Garcia nodded and smiled. "That's good." She pointed to the screen. "You know, Sam, I haven't gotten anything from you in a while."

"I know, I know." I stared at the screen. It was filled

with numbers and symbols. None of it made any sense. I'd never felt so dumb in a math class. "I'll have something tomorrow."

She smiled at me. "It is a challenge, isn't it?" And she looked so pleased with herself, so happy that she'd found a way to make Sam Pettigrew even more miserable.

I reached out and clicked off the monitor. "It's not that it's so challenging," I said. "It's just . . . you know . . . if I didn't have . . . " And I came that close to saying, "if I didn't have Max." I took a deep breath and stared down at my fingers, resting on the keyboard. "If I didn't have so much to do, I'd be able to actually think about this stuff."

She stood up and put her hand on my shoulder. "Just let me know if you need any help."

That night, I was trying to simultaneously spoon mashed peas into Max and read my government text when the phone rang.

"Hey. It's me," Claire said.

"Hey," I said. I cradled the phone between my shoulder and my ear and shoved the jar of peas away. "How's it going?"

"Good. Listen. I had this great idea."

I liked that about Claire. That she pretty much always just got to the point. "What's the idea?" I leaned over and started wiping Max off with a wet washcloth.

"I was thinking we should take Max and Emily to the rhododendron gardens. This Saturday."

I wiped peas out of Max's ear. "Take them where?"

"The rhododendron gardens. They're incredible. All these windy paths through these great old rhodies. And this huge pond."

Max had grabbed the washcloth and was sucking on it. If people stared when it was just Max and me, what would it be like with Emily and Claire there, too? "It's October. There won't be any flowers." Even I knew the whole point of rhododendrons was the flowers.

"Sam, Sam. Of course there won't be flowers. But there will be ducks!"

"Ducks?" I laughed, she said it so funny. Max looked at me, and he smiled around the washcloth.

"Lots of ducks. The kids will love it."

I was willing to bet that a big fat old duck could come along and sit right on top of Emily's head, and she wouldn't know the difference. Max threw the washcloth onto the floor and laughed and looked to see if I was laughing. Max would like ducks. "You're sure about the ducks?"

"I guarantee ducks," Claire said. And I knew she was grinning. I could see the way she was grinning.

"Okay then," I said, and I was grinning, too.

Behind me, the door to the garage opened, and Dad walked in.

"So," I said, "thanks for calling." And I hung up.

"Who was that?" Dad was standing there, wiping his dirty hands on a rag.

I stood up, picked up the washcloth, and handed it back to Max. "Nobody," I said. "Just a kid from school."

When Claire and Emily showed up on Saturday, I had Max all ready to go. I'd stuffed my backpack with diapers and bottles. I'd dug the stroller Aunt Connie had given us out of the garage and wiped off the dust and cobwebs.

Claire jumped out of the driver's seat as I carried Max out. "Hey guys. Isn't it a beautiful day?" She raised her arms and tipped her head back to the sun. She was wearing a purple University of Washington sweatshirt and tight new-looking jeans. She looked good.

"It's a great day," I said, and Max shrieked and waved both hands at her.

I was kind of hoping we'd just go, not hang around or anything. But I had to move Max's car seat from the Datsun to the VW, and that took longer than I expected. I had trouble anchoring it down properly. Emily was already strapped into her car seat. She watched me struggle and swear under my breath, and she gave me one of her vague, dreamy smiles.

"She likes you," Claire said. She was holding Max. "She admires your expertise with a car seat."

"Sure she does," I said, and I swore, very softly, at the friggin' stupid idiots who'd designed this total piece of . . . Finally I got it fastened in.

I straightened up and saw Dad standing on the front porch.

Claire saw him, too. "Oh. You must be Mr. Pettigrew." She crossed up the walk, moving Max to her left arm, holding out her hand. "I'm Claire Bailey."

"Ah," Dad said. He shook her hand.

"We're taking the babies to look at ducks." She tickled Max. "You'll like ducks, won't you, Max?"

Dad looked at her and Max. Then he looked over them at me. "Know when you'll be back?"

"I'm not sure."

"Not late," Claire said. "Emily has an extremely short attention span, even for a three-month-old."

"Because I'm going over to Ted's later," Dad said to me. "Help him with that tree that came down."

"Okay," I said.

"Wasn't that wind something? Last weekend? I thought the roof was going to come off," Claire said.

Dad looked down at her. "Well," he said. He looked at me. "So I'll see you later." And he went back in the house.

Claire brought Max around the VW. "He's kind of quiet, isn't he? Your dad."

"Yeah." I stood there, looking at the closed front door. I knew what he was thinking. Sam and a girl. But he'd never specifically said I couldn't go out. That wasn't part of our deal.

Claire drove almost like a guy, smooth on the gears, a little over the speed limit on the freeway. When a jerk in a pickup cut in front of her, she swore at him and flipped him off. "You learn that on the debate team?" I asked.

She grinned. "First lesson." She checked the babies in the rearview mirror. "They didn't notice, did they?"

Max was trying to jam the entire left sleeve of his

jacket into his mouth. Emily looked like she was asleep. "I don't think they noticed," I said.

The rhododendron gardens were way in southeast Portland. A neighborhood I'd never seen before. Claire parked in the gravel lot, and we dug out all the strollers and the bags and the babies. Emily had a real state-of-the-art stroller, with a cover and everything. Claire strapped her in, then stood up.

I was fumbling with Max's stroller. For some reason, it wouldn't open all the way. Claire reached over and flipped a bracket on the wheel. The stroller popped open. "That gets stuck all the time," I said.

She nodded and smiled.

Max was pumped, you could tell. He leaned out of the stroller, trying to grab twigs and pebbles and Emily. He was babbling, making just about every sound he knew, and pointing at things.

An old lady was selling duck food by the entrance gate. We stopped so Claire could buy some. The lady leaned over her table and smiled down at Emily and Max. "What beautiful babies," she said. She looked at Claire and me. "Are you two baby-sitting?"

"Yes," I nearly blurted out, but Claire said, "Oh, no. They're ours."

"Yours?" The woman's eyebrows went up, and you could see her working it out. "Oh," she said. Then, "Oh," she said again. She looked at me and frowned.

I headed off down the path. Claire jogged to catch up. "What's wrong?"

"Nothing."

Claire shook her head. "Who cares what she thinks, Sam? She's just an old lady selling duck food." She pushed Emily's stroller in front of me. "Come on. Race you to the pond."

The pond was big. A small lake. On the other side was a golf course. You could see guys in ugly sweaters and uglier hats, teeing off. There was a wooden bridge that crossed over to an island in the middle of the water. Two ducks circled over and landed with a splash about ten feet away from us. Max screamed and laughed.

We bumped the strollers onto the bridge and crossed over to the island. There were more bushes and plants over there, but we found a bench, near the water, and Claire and I sat down with the strollers in front of us.

A little flock of ducks swam over. They all started quacking, hoping for a handout. Max leaned forward as far as he could. "Quack!" the ducks shouted. "Bap! Bap!" Max shouted back.

"He's bilingual," Claire said. "He talks duck."

"Bap!" Max shouted louder, and, just for a second, the ducks all shut up.

"I guess he does," I said. Sometimes—I'd never told anybody this—but sometimes Max seemed pretty dumb to me. I worried about it a little. But now, with Claire and Emily, he seemed pretty smart. Pretty hip and aware. I reached down and tickled him, and he shrieked.

Emily was lying back in her stroller. She had dark hair, like Claire's, and the same big brown eyes. You could see she was going to be pretty someday. I wondered what Trent looked like.

"You think she's warm enough?" Claire asked, fumbling at the blanket on Emily's lap.

The sun was shining right on us. I had unzipped my jacket. "She's fine," I said.

Claire dug into her bag and pulled out the bag of duck food. She flung a handful out into the water, and, immediately, the ducks multiplied by five. You couldn't see the water for ducks. Max shrieked and clapped his hands.

"I absolutely had to get out of the house," Claire said. "My mother drives me crazy on weekends." She looked at me. "Your mom's dead, isn't she?" She asked it like it wasn't sad or weird. Like it was something that was just sort of interesting about me.

I watched the ducks. "Yeah. She had cancer, when I was in fourth grade." I wasn't sure that I'd ever said it like that before, right out like that. I looked at Claire. "How did you know?"

"Oh, somebody told me. Back in middle school." She smiled. "I asked around about you."

"You did?"

"Yeah, I did." And we sat there, smiling at each other.

"Bap!" Max yelled at the ducks. "Bap! Bap!"

Claire leaned back on the bench. "Does your dad help you out with Max?"

"Well. You know. I'm lucky. Max is a laid-back guy. I don't need a lot of help. I've got it under control."

"But your dad could give you a hand."

"No. It's not . . . Dad's great. Max is my responsibility." Max was leaning forward, straining against the straps.

Trying to catch a duck. And I remembered a night back in August. Max screaming in his crib and me sitting in the bathroom, counting to 1,000 by 13's because nothing else was working. And somewhere around 429, I realized Max wasn't screaming anymore. I realized he was laughing. And I heard Dad talking, talking in this goofy voice, and Max laughing harder. "I think," I said, "he likes Max."

Claire sighed. "And meanwhile, at my house, I have to fight to even get to hold Emily." She tipped her chin down into the neck of her sweatshirt. "I leave her at day care all day, and then I get home, and Natalie wants to play with her, and my dad wants to take her for a walk, and my grandmother begs to change her diaper."

I laughed, and then I saw she wasn't laughing.

She tipped her head down even farther. "Last night my mother and I were screaming, screaming at each other about rice cereal." She pulled her head up. Her eyes were swimming with tears. She looked at me like I should say something. Do something.

I leaned over and put my arms around her, and I kissed her. Her lips were soft and warm, and she put her arms around me and kissed me back.

"Bap!" Max yelled.

MARGARET BECHARD

chapter thirteen

I HAVEN'T BEEN TO the hospital since I was nine years old. It takes me a long time to find Room 708. Because I'm too embarrassed to ask directions.

There are two beds in the room. The one nearest the door is empty. Brittany is in the one by the window. She looks asleep.

I haven't seen Brittany since last August, since the last of our "discussions" with her parents and my dad.

She opens her eyes as I step into the room. "Oh. Hi."

I stay in the doorway. "Your mom called me. Last night."

"I know."

I look around the room. I'm not sure how this works. "Where is he?"

"He's in the nursery. They think I'll faint or something. I did, almost, this morning. I had a hard delivery, you know."

"Your mom said." I wince a little, remembering how her mom had said it. "She said it was fast, though."

"Oh, right. Easy for her to say."

I walk closer to the bed. "You look . . . great." Which isn't totally true. I've never seen Brittany with no make-up and clumpy hair.

Something rattles in the doorway. A nurse, wearing bright pink pants and a flowered shirt, wheels in a clear plastic box. There's a bundle of blankets inside. "Feeding time," the nurse says. She stops when she sees me. "And who's this?"

I open and shut my mouth.

"He's the father," Brittany says.

"Well, hi, Dad!" the nurse says. "Good to see you!" And she sounds like she is happy to see me. "Let's introduce you to your son."

I take a step backward.

She bends down and picks up the bundle of blankets. "Sit down in that chair there."

MARGARET BECHARD

I take another step, and my legs hit a chair seat. I sit down. "I thought . . . isn't he hungry?"

"He can wait a few minutes. Meeting Dad is pretty important, too." The nurse stands in front of me, eyeing me up and down. "You play football?"

"Yeah. Sort of. Third string. Lot of time on the bench." I'm babbling, but I can't seem to stop.

"Good. Because it's pretty much like holding a football. Just more wiggly. Now crook your left arm a little."

I do what she tells me, and she settles the blankets— the baby—into my arms. There's a little face, red and wrinkled, sticking out of the top. He's wearing a blue knit hat, and his hands are covered with little mittens, like he's about to go skiing or something. Holding him does not feel anything like holding a football.

The blood is singing in my ears. The nurse puts her hand on my shoulder. "Take a breath, there, Dad. A good deep breath." I do, and I feel a little better. She smiles. "You've got to remember to take deep breaths."

"He's really little," I whisper.

"Seven pounds, six ounces," the nurse says. "Just about perfect. Mom did a great job." She squeezes my shoulder. "You hang on there while I get Mom organized."

She moves over to Brittany, and I hear the motor on the bed, raising the head up. I stare down at the baby. His eyes are shut, and his mouth is scrunched into a tight little bunch. I want to ask if that red color is normal. I want to ask if he can open his eyes yet, because maybe it's like puppies and kittens . . . And, just as I think that, his eyes do open. They're a color I've never seen before, a watery blue-gray. No real color at all. He looks surprised to see me. His mouth opens, too, like it's connected to his eyes, and he gives a sudden sharp, loud cry.

I nearly drop him.

The nurse hurries over. "Just in time," she says. "Good job, Dad. Mom's all ready."

She holds out her arms, and, I don't know why, but my hands tighten on him. Even though he's funny-looking and scary. But I hand him to her.

She carries him over to Brittany and stays, bent over the bed. It takes me a minute, but then I figure it out. She's breastfeeding him. The nurse whispers, "He needs to take the whole thing." And Brittany says, "But it hurts." They're so intense, so focused. It reminds me of the time Andy and I tried to fix the engine on his radio-controlled car.

It's not like I've never seen Brittany's breasts. And then it seems wrong to be even thinking about her breasts. The nurse straightens up. She looks triumphant. "Look at him suck!" she says.

I go over to the window. They're building a new parking garage, and there's a crane out there, carrying girders back and forth. Behind me, I can hear these gross baby eating noises. After a long time, the nurse says, "Good work, Mom. Now pat his back. Try to burp him."

I turn around. Brittany is all covered up, holding the baby on her shoulder. The blankets are gone. In just a diaper and T-shirt he looks—well—like a little mutant. His head's enormous, and his arms and legs are amazingly spindly. Brittany's hand covers almost his whole back.

The nurse smiles at me. "Seeing as how Dad's here, I'll leave you guys alone for a bit." She bustles out.

Nobody says anything. Brittany holds the baby against her shoulder. It looks awkward, and I want to suggest that maybe if she moved her hand down a little . . . but I'm afraid to say anything. Finally, I say, "So. How's the alternative school thing?"

She sighs. "I don't know. I think it's an okay school. But I feel weird there." She shifts her hand, and the baby's head wobbles. I want to take him from her, but I don't know if I'm allowed to hold him standing up.

Mrs. Ames walks in. She frowns at me. "Oh," she says. And then, to Brittany, "What's wrong?"

"Nothing's wrong, Mom," Brittany says. "Everything's fine. I just fed him, and now I'm going to change him." She starts to swing her legs over the side of the bed.

"I'll do it," Mrs. Ames says. She takes the baby, puts him back in the box, and starts undoing the diaper. He cries again, a loud, outraged squeal. "Oh, don't make such a fuss," Mrs. Ames mutters.

Brittany looks at me. "So," she says, "I bet *your* dad is glad to be a grandparent."

Actually, I haven't told him. "Oh, yeah," I say.

Mrs. Ames sticks on a new diaper. "Tell him his share of the bill is coming."

"Right." The diaper looks way too big for the little body. "I got a job at the plumbing store," I say, more to the baby than anybody. "I'm paying my dad back."

"And warn him it's more than we expected," Mrs. Ames says. She's looking for a clean shirt and blankets.

MARGARET BECHARD

"I'll tell him," I say.

Mrs. Ames puts the baby in Brittany's arms. Then she sits in the chair, my chair. Out in the hall, someone's talking. A baby cries. A man laughs. Suddenly I feel too big for this room. Like I'm taking up too much space.

I clear my throat. "So. Have you picked a name?"

"Julian Patrick Ames," Brittany says.

"Julian," I say.

"It's a nice name," Brittany says, frowning at me. "Like Julian Lennon."

I want to say it's a fruity name. I want to say that, in sixth grade, he's going to hate that name. But I don't think I can say anything.

"Can you lower my head a little?" Brittany says.

Mrs. Ames doesn't move, so I say, "Sure." I find the controls and lower the head of the bed. For just a second, I wonder if Brittany knows all the things this bed can do. How the head and foot can go up and down. But she looks too tired. She bends her face back down to the baby. To Julian. Mrs. Ames looks out the window.

Nobody notices when I leave the room.

chapter **fourteen**

CLAIRE AND I KISSED again in the VW in the driveway at my house. Max and Emily, exhausted by ducks, asleep in their car seats. Dad's truck still gone.

I had to lean over the gearshift and scrunch around the steering wheel. It was complicated and uncomfortable.

But I'd missed kissing, too.

At 10:30 that night, Claire called. We talked for over an hour. I had to keep my voice down. So I wouldn't wake up Max, flat on his back in the crib next to me. Or Dad. I didn't want to wake up Dad, either.

The next Wednesday was Halloween. I knew it as soon as I walked into the day care because the secretary was dressed as Big Bird and Mrs. Aldritch, the two-year-olds' teacher, was The Cat in the Hat.

Mrs. Aldritch smiled at me. "Ready for the costume parade, Sam?"

Mrs. McPherson came out of the changing room with Tyler. She was dressed as a gypsy. Or maybe a homeless person. Tyler was Cookie Monster. Mrs. McPherson must have seen the look on my face. "We take the kids around to the other classrooms. The big kids love it. I mean, the teenaged big kids," she added, and Mrs. Aldritch laughed. "I mentioned it on Monday, Sam. Remember?"

If I'd remembered, I'd have stayed home.

I looked through the door to the crawlers room. Kristin and Augusto were both Teletubbies. Gemma was a witch. I looked at Max. Halloween. I couldn't even do Halloween.

"Sam!" Claire came in with Emily and all her stuff. Claire was wearing bell bottoms, a fringed poncho, and a headband. "I'm a hippy!" she said.

"I can tell," I said. And I thought, why didn't you remind me? And then I felt bad. Like Claire's supposed to take care of me.

"Great costume," Mrs. Aldritch said.

"It's my mom's stuff." Claire shoved me with her diaper bag. "You and Max, come with me."

We followed her into the changing room. "Trade babies," she said. She handed me Emily and took Max. She plunked him down on one of the changing tables.

Emily was a lion. She had a hooded lion suit, with a mane of yellow-and-brown yarn framing her face. When I turned her over, she even had a tail. I turned her back upright. "You're pretty darn cute." She gave me a big toothless lion smile.

Claire was rummaging in her backpack. "Ta-da!" She pulled out a hideously bright yellow sweatshirt. "I saw this, and I knew it was Max."

"Geez, Claire. I don't know. I think Max prefers blue, or maybe black?"

She waved the shirt at me. "No. See. It's a duck!"

The hood of the sweatshirt had a big bill and goofy eyes and a tuft of feathers sticking out of the top. I laughed. "I don't know if he'll wear that."

But she was already pulling off his jacket and tugging the thing over Max's head. He didn't even squirm and fight. "You're a duck, Max," she said. "Quack, quack."

"Bap! Bap!" Max said, right back, and Emily shrieked.

Claire dug in her bag again and pulled out a black mask. The plastic kind that just goes over your eyes. "I

MARGARET BECHARD

got this for you, Sam. You know. Sort of subtle and understated. By day, mild-mannered teenage dad. By night, Mystery Man!"

I grinned. I liked that. "It's great. You're . . ." Quick, before anybody could come in, I leaned over and kissed her.

I carried Max in the costume parade, and he "bap-bapped" the whole way. People seemed to get the joke, and they laughed. Ms. Garcia took him from me and stood him on her desk, and he bapped at her whole class. It was probably the best I'd ever felt at that school.

Claire's VW was parked next to the Datsun, and she was strapping Emily into her car seat at the end of school. I put Max in his seat, and then brought the sweatshirt around. "Here," I said. "It was a big hit."

"I know. I heard him!" She pushed the shirt back at me. "Keep it. It's definitely Max."

"Thanks." And then, like I didn't have to say anything or do anything, she just stepped toward me, and I wrapped my arms around her. She pressed against me, her head nestling into the space between my jaw and my shoulder. I'd forgotten . . . I'd forgotten how girls just kind of fit. I tightened my arms, and she wrapped hers around me.

"I like you, Sam Pettigrew," she said, softly, her breath warm against my neck.

"Yeah. I like you, too," I said.

She called again that night. Late. I'd been trying to do some of the math, but the equations just kept jumbling around.

"Hi," she said. Softly. Like maybe Emily was asleep, too.

"Hi." I wiggled past the crib and lay down on my bed. Claire could talk a lot, on the phone. I didn't have to say much. I closed my eyes, letting her voice slide into my head, and I was your typical seventeen-year-old guy talking to a girl he liked. A girl he'd kissed in her car. A girl he'd hugged in the parking lot.

"You know what I was thinking?" Claire asked, suddenly.

I opened my eyes. My mind pinballed around all the things she could be thinking and all the things I had been thinking. "What?" I asked, finally.

"I think we should take the kids to the mall on Saturday."

"To the mall?" There was one thing I hadn't thought of.

MARGARET BECHARD

"Yeah. My grandfather sent me some money. And there's a sale at Baby Gap."

It would be packed, packed with staring people. "It'll be really crowded on Saturday. And we'll never be able to park."

"Sam. Do you have anything else planned?"

If Max went with the schedule, if he napped in the afternoon, I planned to be on the couch, asleep. "No. Nothing exactly planned."

"So. It'll be good for you to get out."

And, just for a second, I felt—not that Claire wasn't great, the duck costume, the garden—it was all great . . .

"It'll be good for Max, too," she added.

If I put off the haircut for one more week . . . "We can eat lunch at Taco Bell. There's one in the food court."

Claire laughed, and I heard Emily start to cry. "Oh, hell," Claire said. "What time is it?"

"A little after midnight."

"Damn. I was hoping . . ." Emily's cry turned to a wail. In the background Mrs. Bailey said something. "I gotta go. See you tomorrow." And Claire hung up.

I pushed the power button on the phone and dropped it on the floor.

A shadow in the doorway broke away from the surrounding darkness. Dad stepped into the light.

"Holy . . ." I jumped and banged my head, hard, against the headboard. "Ow, ow ow!"

Max jerked awake and started to cry.

I leaned over, one hand on my head, and reached down with the other hand to pat Max's back. "Shh, shh."

"Who were you talking to?"

I rubbed my head and patted Max a little harder. "Claire. You know. The girl . . . the girl who came over." I wondered how long he'd been standing there.

Max was quieting, going back to sleep.

"Are you having sex with her, Sam?"

"What?" I couldn't believe he'd said that. "No," I said, my voice loud. Max jerked again, but didn't open his eyes. I turned and looked at Dad. "We were just talking. I can't even talk to a girl on the phone?"

"You have to be careful, Sam," he said. Not looking at me. Looking at Max.

"I know that," I said. "Don't you think I know that? We're not . . . it's not anything like that. Not at all."

"I just don't . . ." He crossed his arms across his chest. "You have to *think*, Sam."

I know that, too. "Look," I said. "You don't . . . you don't have to worry. I'm sorry I woke you up."

"I wasn't asleep," he said. And he turned and went back into the dark hallway.

I turned off my light and lay back down on my bed. *You have to think, Sam.* It seemed like all I did was think. Because everything in my life, every single thing, was so hard to figure out. School. Claire. Dad. Max. And it wasn't like I'd thought it was going to be easy. But at least I thought it was going to feel right.

Max stirred, whimpered. Then he started to cry. I swore, clicked on the light, and picked him up.

chapter fifteen

DAD WAS GONE WHEN Max and I got up on Saturday morning. He'd left a note on the table. "Fishing," it said.

Only diehard crazies went out in November. But I looked out the window, and it was another great day. The sun shining again. Cold, maybe, but it would be beautiful out on the river.

And I wished I was out there with him. And I wondered if he'd even want me along.

Claire and Emily showed up at 11:00, and we drove to the mall in the VW.

It took us twenty-five minutes to find a parking space.

I flipped open Max's stroller in the parking lot and buckled him in. No fumbling. Piece of cake. Max grinned and blew spit bubbles at Claire.

She didn't even notice. She was holding a piece of blue fabric with lots of buckles and straps. "It's a front pack to carry Emily," she said. "My mom got it. She read this thing about how babies who are carried around do better."

"Do better than what?" Would Emily be better than Max?

Claire shook her head. "My *mom* read the article, not me." She turned the thing around. "I don't know how this is supposed to work."

"Did it come with instructions?"

"Yes."

"Did you read them?"

She looked at me. "I figured . . . " She frowned at the pack. "How hard can this be?"

"We could just use your stroller."

"I didn't bring the friggin' stroller, okay, Sam?" Claire's voice echoed off the cement walls of the parking structure. "I just brought this! Because my stupid mother said it's better! Okay?"

"Okay," I said. "Calm down. Let's figure it out."

After a lot of fumbling and swearing, and Max and Emily both getting pissed off and cranky, we got Emily into the pack. She didn't look real comfortable, but she was in there.

The mall was packed. People were staring.

Claire cheered up in Baby Gap. She held up an outfit—a little tiny pair of jeans and a little tiny jeans jacket. "What do you think? Is this Emily?"

"I guess."

"There's a hat that goes with it."

"Of course."

Claire frowned. "What's wrong?"

I shrugged. The outfit cost as much as two tanks of gas for the Datsun. Three even. "Nothing." Max had leaned out of the stroller and was trying to knock over a display of dresses. "I think maybe we'll wait by the cash register."

I pushed Max over to a relatively clear area. While we waited, I watched a mom—way older than Claire, probably as old as Aunt Jean—arguing with her little girl over a party dress. "Miranda. You have to be reasonable," the mom kept saying. And Miranda kept screaming, "I want it! I want it now!"

And I had this flash of me and Max someday. Max wanting something like cool shoes. I could imagine that.

Hell. I wanted cool shoes. And I imagined me arguing with the future pissed-off Max, him mad at me, probably hating me.

My head started to ache.

When Claire was finally done, she grinned at me. "Time for Taco Bell, huh, big guy?"

"Right," I said.

Taco Bell was crowded, too, but we managed to snag a table in the back corner. There was a family at the table next to us, a mom and dad and two little kids. The mom was watching Claire and me.

Max was happy in a high chair, mushing together some rice and bits of chicken from my chalupa. But Emily was having a fit. She was crying in the front pack, twisting her head, screaming.

"She's hungry," Claire said. She was trying to eat a taco and rock and pat Emily at the same time.

I'd already finished my chalupa and my two burritos. And I was feeling a little better. "I could hold her," I said, "if it would help."

"Let's try." Claire stood up, and we started unfastening the straps and buckles. Emily screamed even louder.

"Can I help?" It was the mom from the next table. "I

used to have one of these." Somehow, in about two seconds, she had Emily out. "Here you go."

I took Emily from her, and, amazingly, she shut up and sort of burrowed into my shirt.

Claire sat down. "What a relief."

The woman patted Emily's back and smiled at me. "You have a beautiful family."

I opened my mouth, but Claire said, "Oh, thank you," before I could get any words out. "Of course, they're a handful, two so close together."

"I can imagine," the woman said, still smiling. She patted Emily again. "You take good care of her, Dad." She went back to her table.

Claire was eating her taco and grinning. I frowned. I leaned forward and whispered, "You know what she thinks?"

"Oh, let her think it. It's funny." Claire gave Max some more rice. "Don't you think it's funny?"

Emily was sucking on my shirt, leaving a big wet patch. "It's embarrassing."

"We haven't done anything wrong. We don't have anything to be embarrassed about, Sam." Claire finished her taco and stood up, dusting tortilla crumbs off her jeans. "There's this great bathroom in Nordstrom's. It has couches and a changing table. I can feed her there. And it's a family bathroom. You guys can come, too."

"No." I glanced over at the mom. She was still smiling at us. I handed Emily over. "We'll wait by the skating rink."

"Give us about twenty minutes." Claire hustled off, Emily screaming on her shoulder.

I cleared off the table. Then I got Max back into the stroller and went to find a men's room.

Of course there was no changing table. But the floor was pretty clean. I spread my jacket out and plunked Max down on it. Fortunately he was just wet.

I dressed him and put him back in the stroller. I sort of had to go to the bathroom, too, but it seemed like too much hassle.

I pushed Max around by the skating rink. I gave him a bottle of juice, and he sat there, sucking down apple juice and watching the people walk by.

A bunch of little kids were playing hockey on the rink. An old couple, Dad's age, were watching. The woman kept pounding on the glass and shouting, "Go Rangers! Go Kyle!" at the top of her lungs.

I looked down at Max. He'd fallen asleep, his mouth still hanging onto the bottle, his head crooked to one side. I eased the bottle away without waking him up and stuck it back in the diaper bag.

Claire showed up about thirty minutes later. Emily was sound asleep, her head bobbing against Claire's chest. Claire grinned. "A woman helped me put her back in. It turned out we had one of the straps fastened wrong."

"Good," I said.

Claire sighed and frowned. "Sam. What is wrong? You've been acting weirded out ever since we got here."

"I'm great. I'm fine. I've just got a headache." Which was true.

"Hey! Look who's here!" Andy came up behind me. "How's it going, dude?" He was holding hands with Jenny.

My head throbbed. "Andy." I took a step back and waved my hand at Claire. "It's Andy, again," I said. "And this is Jenny."

"I know Claire," Jenny said. I hadn't seen Jenny in a long time. She'd cut her hair short and dyed it purplish black. It looked good. "Is this your baby?" She put her free hand, gently, on Emily's head. "What's her . . . his name?"

"Emily," Claire said.

"What a doll," Jenny said. "Isn't she a doll, Andy?"

"*You* have a baby, too?" Andy said. He had that pop-eyed cartoon look again.

"Andy." Jenny shoved him with her shoulder. "For heaven's sake."

Claire was smiling. "You must have heard the rumors, Andy. I'm sure it was all over school."

"Yeah, but." Andy shrugged. "I didn't believe them."

Claire reached out and put her hand on his arm. "Smart girls get pregnant, too, Andy. Trust me, I was as shocked as you are." She laughed, and, after a couple of seconds, so did Andy.

Jenny was bending down over the stroller. "And this is Max?" He was still zonked.

"Yeah. That's Max."

"He's bigger than he was," Andy said. "Since that time at your house." He looked at me. "Remember?"

"Yeah."

Andy looked at Jenny and Claire. "I went over one day after school, and Max like threw up all over everything. The couch, the rug. Sam. It was a houseful of puke."

Jenny and Claire both laughed.

"It wasn't that bad," I said.

"Ooh, boy," Andy said. "It was bad enough for me."

"How old is Max?" Jenny asked. She was still crouched down in front of him.

"Eleven months," I said.

"Almost a year," Claire said, at the same time.

We looked at each other. Then I nodded. "Yeah. That's right. Almost a year."

Jenny stood up. She gave Andy another nudge. "We were going for coffee," Andy said. "You guys want to come?"

Claire raised her eyebrows at me. "Okay," I said. "Coffee would be okay." More to her than to them. And I was figuring how much cash I had left. I didn't want Claire to buy her own drink. Not in front of Jenny and Andy.

"Yes!" the hockey mother shrieked. "Way to go, Kyle!" She started rhythmically pounding the glass.

Jenny rolled her eyes. "Let's go to the Starbuck's down by Penney's. Where it's quieter."

Jenny and Claire walked together down the mall, their heads close, talking. Andy and I walked behind them. I had to keep maneuvering the stroller away from Jenny's heels.

Andy glanced over at me. "You and Claire, huh? Together at last?"

I sighed. "It's not like that. We're just friends."

He nodded. "Right." We were quiet, past Sharper Image and Track and Trail. "I like this thing you've got going with your hair," Andy said. "The curls and all."

"Andy. Shut up."

He laughed.

I was really glad to see the Starbuck's. I had just enough money to buy Claire's mocha and a small latte for me. We took the drinks over to one of the benches. Claire and Jenny and I sat down. I don't know if it was the caffeine or just Andy's usual short attention span, but he stood in front of us, and he was the old Andy again, jazzed up, talking a mile a minute, clearly not thinking about babies anymore. He did a play-by-play of their last football game, acting out the players on both teams.

Max woke up halfway through, and I gave him the rest of his bottle. He sat there, sucking away and staring, very seriously, at Andy.

"And there was a long pass," Andy said. "Six seconds

to go . . . and Trevor caught it." He pillowed his hand, softly, in Max's lap, as if Max were this Trevor guy, as if Max had made the play. "And we won the game!" Max laughed, apple juice dribbling down his chin and his neck. Andy laughed, too. Then he sniffed. "Somebody," he said, straightening up and pointing a thumb at Max, "does not smell so sweet."

"Oh . . ." I stood up. "I gotta find a men's room."

"There's one in Penney's," Claire said. She stood up, too.

Jenny tossed her empty cup into the trash. "We gotta go, anyway. I have to find something for my mom's birthday."

Andy held out his arm, and Jenny snuggled up against him. "We should do something sometime," Andy said. He waved his free hand. "All of us."

Claire stepped closer to me, and after a second, I put my arm around her. "Sounds like fun," she said. She looked up at me.

I tightened my arm on her shoulder. "Sure," I said. "Sounds great."

chapter sixteen

BRITTANY'S MOM CALLS ABOUT two weeks after I visit the hospital. "Let me talk to your father," she says.

Dad's in his room, reading. I stand in the doorway. "Yes," he says. "Yes. Well . . ." He glances at me, then away. "I'll talk to him."

I go back in the living room and sit on the couch. It's Wednesday. There's nothing on TV on Wednesday.

Dad comes in. He's wearing an old pair of jeans, torn out at both knees, and a faded T-shirt that says "Pettigrew Electric" on the pocket.

"If it's the hospital bill," I say, "I already talked to Mike about maybe adding more hours at work. Maybe Saturday morning . . ."

He walks over and clicks off the TV. "They're giving the baby up for adoption after all."

I just sit there and stare at him.

He shakes his head. "I don't know why they're saying this now. I mean, after all the discussions we had, and they were absolutely so positive." He sounds mad, like they're doing this just to annoy him.

"Does Brittany know?" As soon as I say it, I know it's stupid. But I can't get my head around this. She's changed her mind?

Dad frowns at me. "I'm sure she knows, Sam."

"I mean . . . well, do you think it's her idea?"

"Sam. Mrs. Ames just said she thought we should know. That's all she said."

I cut school the next day, and I go over to Brittany's. I know she's home because she doesn't have to go to school until the baby's at least four weeks old. And I know her mom and dad have left for work.

I just want to talk to her. I just want to understand what's going on.

I stop at Starbuck's on the way over. I haven't seen her and the baby—her and Julian—since that day at the hospital. But I've been thinking about them a lot.

I've been thinking about him and how he looked when he opened his eyes so suddenly. Surprised to see me.

I can tell Brittany's surprised to see me, too. "Sam."

"Hi."

She looks beyond me, at the Datsun in the driveway, like she thinks maybe I'm not alone.

I hold up the coffee. "Want an iced nonfat raspberry mocha?"

She looks from me to the drink and back at me. Then she shrugs and steps aside, letting me in.

I go into the living room. "You look . . ." I nearly say "better," but I stop myself. Although she does look better. She's wearing makeup, and her hair is fancy, pulled back in lots of tiny beaded braids to the top of her head, and then falling down all around her shoulders. She's not as skinny as she was, but she doesn't look like she's ever been pregnant. "You look great," I say, and I hand her the drink.

"Thanks." She sits down on the big white couch facing the windows.

"Uh . . . where's Julian?" For a second, I think maybe he's already gone.

She points at a basket-thing near the window. "He's asleep. Don't wake him up."

I walk over, softly, and peer into the basket. "Whoa," I whisper. "He's gotten bigger." Not like he's huge or anything. He's still amazingly small. But definitely not the same worm baby I saw in the hospital. Definitely coming along.

Brittany doesn't say anything. I turn around. She's sipping the mocha carefully, her lips barely touching the straw.

I take a drink of my vanilla latte. It's gotten cold on the drive over, and the sweetness clogs my tongue. I clear my throat. "I've been meaning to call. Or come over. So I could help out. Maybe do . . ." My brain clogs, too. I can't think of anything I could possibly do. "Something," I finish.

She puts her cup down on the table. "That's nice of you, Sam. I mean, really. I know . . ." She waves her hand, like she can't say everything she knows. Like it's all just out there somewhere, beyond her reach. "But it wouldn't make any difference. I'd still give him up." And she smiles at me, a real smile, like she used to smile, back when she liked me. And, just for a second, my stomach tightens, remembering how it was.

I sit down in the armchair. "I thought you'd . . .

MARGARET BECHARD

we'd . . . I thought you'd decided to keep him."

She sighs. She's sitting perfectly straight on the couch, her back not touching the cushions behind her, her feet and knees and hands all pressed together. "I knew," she says, staring down at the mocha, "I knew right from the beginning that I wasn't going to have an abortion. I always knew I didn't want that. And I knew I wasn't . . . I knew I didn't want to get married." She shoots me a look, and I nod and blush. I remember that conversation pretty well. "I truly thought I knew everything else, too." Brittany leans forward a little and makes a face, like maybe her stomach aches. "You were here, right? When we talked about adoption?"

I nod again. Dad and I had both been here. We'd sat on that couch. And we'd listened to Brittany and her parents talk. They'd talked a lot.

"My mom," Brittany says now, "you know, she always was big on it." She shakes her head and rolls her eyes. Her hands are trembling. "There was even . . . my dad's sister lives in Los Angeles, and we even talked about me going to stay with her. Have the baby—Julian—down there. Which sounded okay, you know. I mean, don't you think it would be kind of fun? To live in L.A.?" She looks at me.

"Yeah," I say. "Yeah. I was thinking about going to college down there."

She nods. "That's right. I remember that." She picks up the mocha, then puts it back down without taking a drink.

We're both quiet for a few minutes. So quiet, I can hear Julian breathing in the basket.

"You know," she says, "sometimes I think if my mother could just have shut up for like two minutes, instead of constantly telling me what I should do. . . ." She drops her head to her knees, and I can see all the little clean white parts splitting her blond hair and the intricate weaving of the braids. "Anyway," she says, her voice muffled, "the other thing I knew was I wasn't going to just rush into making a decision. I wasn't going to be pushed. I was going to give it—give him—every chance."

I nod, even though she can't see me. Even though I'm not sure exactly what she's saying.

She sits up straight again and looks right at me. And she looks—I don't know—different somehow. "But I do know I can't do this, Sam. It's not what I expected. At all. *I'm* not what I expected." She smiles, a sad little smile. "I know this probably doesn't make a lot of sense to you."

"No. It makes sense. I understand." Which is a lie. It doesn't make sense. I don't understand at all. "But, look. It's only been a couple of weeks. Maybe if . . ."

Her face twists up, and I think she's going to yell at me. But instead she smiles again. "It's been plenty of time, Sam. For me." She sighs and leans back against the cushions. She puts her feet up on the coffee table. "We're moving to Boise."

"Boise?"

"My dad's company has an office there. He's wanted to transfer for a long time, but my mom . . ." She shrugs. "I'll go to a new school. Nobody will ever know. My mom keeps saying that."

"And what happens to the baby?"

"The lawyer found this adoption agency. They say he'll be easy to place. You know, blonde-haired . . ."

"Give him to me," I say it fast and loud, before I can think about it.

She stares at me, her face frozen in a funny startled look. "What?"

"Don't give him to strangers. Give him to me."

She's smiling, a strange, twisted little smile. Like something hurts inside. "Sam. You don't know what you're saying. And what about your dad? He'll have a fit."

I shake my head. Because I do know what I'm saying. And I know I don't want this baby to just go away, disappear, so I never know him. So I never ever see him again. And I don't care about Dad.

I stand up. "I'm his father, Brittany," I say. "I want him."

Dad does have a fit. Of course. He pretty much goes ballistic.

But for once in my life, I know exactly what I'm doing. I know exactly what I want. I know exactly what I have to do.

I think it all through on the drive home. And I call Aunt Jean before I tell Dad. I get her on my side. I plan it all out. Work out all the arguments.

So when Dad says, "Are you crazy? You can't do this. You can't be a father."

I say, "I am a father. That's the reality. You said so. You said I have to take responsibility. You said I couldn't just walk away from this." I pause. "I know it's what Mom would want me to do."

When we talk to the lawyer Aunt Jean finds, the first thing I ask about is changing his name to Max.

chapter **seventeen**

Max and Emily fell asleep again on the drive from the mall to my house. Claire turned toward me, from the driver's seat, and gave me a smile. I thought she was going to kiss me again. We were going to make out again. And I wasn't sure I wanted to.

But she didn't kiss me. Instead she said, "Seeing Andy and Jen kind of weirded me out."

"Yeah. Me too."

She rubbed at a smudge under the rearview mirror. "I used to watch you and Andy, back at Willamette View. You always looked like you were having a pretty good time."

"Yeah. Well. We've been . . . we've known each other since first grade."

She rubbed harder at the smudge. "I used to watch you and Brittany, too. You used to kiss in front of her locker. Before third period."

I tipped my head back against the seat and groaned.

"Did she dump you?" Claire asked.

I thought that was really nice of her. To assume that I wouldn't have done the dumping. "It just wasn't the same anymore. You know, once she was pregnant." Then I was afraid I sounded like a jerk. "You know what I mean."

Claire nudged my leg with her knee. "Were you crushed?"

I looked at her. Crushed? Then I shrugged. "Yeah," I said. "Pretty much." I looked out the windshield at the garage door. It needed paint. "I thought some pretty stupid stuff there for a while. I mean, I asked her to marry me. But she didn't want to. Get married. To me."

Claire shook her head. "That girl is so stupid."

And I thought that was a nice thing to say, too. "Yeah. Well. I think I understand more now, though, than I did back then." I didn't look at Claire. I kept staring at the door. "I can understand how she'd want to go off. Start again. Sort of like a do-over, you know." I grinned at her, to show I was kidding. "Like playing T-ball in second grade. We always got a do-over till we hit the ball."

Claire leaned around the gear shift and put her hand on my leg. "I don't think there are do-overs in real life, Sam."

"Yeah," I said. "I know that."

Max startled, like he'd had a bad dream, and he started to cry. Which woke Emily up.

Claire sighed. "Time to go." She patted my leg. "I'll call you tomorrow night."

We watched Claire and Emily pull out of the driveway, Max and me. Then I took him inside and gave him a bath. Max really liked taking baths. He'd sit in the tub for a long time, splashing around and chewing on the washcloth.

I sat on the toilet seat, and I watched him. He had long, strong legs. Even for a baby. And he was taller than a lot of the other babies. Taller than Tyler or Augusto. Maybe someday he'd want to play hockey.

I thought about the mom, screaming, "Way to go, Kyle!"

I leaned against the back of the toilet, and I thought of all the things I had to do. All the things I couldn't do. All the things I wanted to do.

I thought about Claire saying we hadn't done anything wrong.

Max splashed, hard, and water shot up over his head and onto the floor. He looked at me. "D'oh," he said, exactly like Homer Simpson. "D'oh, d'oh."

"Come on. You're just making a mess now." I stood up and got a towel.

Max was sitting in his high chair, gumming up Ritz crackers, and I was sitting at the kitchen table with my math book and my calculator and my blank notebook when Dad walked in the back door.

"Hey," I said. "How was fishing?"

"Okay." He crossed to the fridge and opened it. He reached for a beer, but Max's bottle was in the way.

He set the bottle on the tray in front of Max. Max picked it up and started drinking. I was expecting Dad to take the beer on into the living room. Or maybe to his bedroom. But he pulled out the chair across from me and sat down at the table. He unscrewed the cap, took a big swallow of beer, then put the cap and bottle down, carefully, side by side in front of him. He smelled like cold fresh air and river water and just a little bit of the beer. He smelled good.

I wanted to ask him if maybe there was some way I could go fishing with him. Next time.

"Sam," he said, "I need to know what you're thinking."

"What?" I said.

His hands flexed. "I need to know what you're thinking, Sam," he said again, slowly this time. Like maybe I didn't speak English. Like maybe I'd understand if he just kept saying it over and over.

"Thinking about what?" I said. And then I thought, maybe he was talking about Claire. He knew I'd gone to the mall with her. I'd told him I was going, and he hadn't said anything then. I felt my face and neck flushing red.

Max was watching us both, his eyes swiveling back and forth from Dad to me, his mouth working hard on the bottle.

Dad reached out to the counter next to the fridge. There was a stack of mail there. Some catalogs and what looked like some bills. I'd been working around it for the past couple of days, not wanting to mess up his organization. He always had an organization. He fished through the pile, one-handed, and pulled out an envelope. He dropped it on the table, on top of my math papers.

Max leaned forward in the high chair, as if he wanted to see this, too.

I recognized the logo of the College Board in the upper corner. "Oh," I said. "That."

"I thought it was a bill." Dad waved his left hand. "Something I needed to pay."

I nodded. I didn't know what to say. "It's not a bill," I said, finally. "I mean, you don't have to pay anything." I looked at Max. He looked at me. "It's my SAT scores."

"I know that, Sam. I know what they are." He rocked the beer bottle back and forth. "Are you thinking you're going to college?"

I took a breath and looked at him. I wanted to say, "No, of course I'm not thinking I'm going to college." I wanted to say, "I'm going to go work for Mr. Lawson. Like we planned all along." Only none of that stuff would come out. I just took another breath and shook my head.

"Because, Sam . . ." I could tell he was getting mad. The way his hands clenched, the way he shifted in his chair. Someday Max would be able to tell when I was mad. "I just don't know what you're thinking."

There was the sound of footsteps in the garage. Someone fumbled at the door. All three of us turned.

The door opened, and Aunt Jean walked in. She was carrying two bulging canvas tote bags. "The garage door was open, so I just came on through." She smiled at us.

Max immediately dropped the bottle and held out his hands toward her. "Bah-bah," he said.

She set the bags down and walked over and picked him up. "Hello, pumpkin." She looked at Dad and me. "I brought over some chili. I made way too much for Ted and me. We'd be eating it for a month. And I found some spaghetti sauce at the back of the freezer." She stopped and hoisted Max a little higher in her arms. "What's wrong?" She looked at Dad.

He flicked the envelope with his finger. "It seems Sam here thinks he's going to college."

She looked at me. "You got your test scores back?"

I nodded.

"How did you do?"

I shrugged.

"You knew about this, Jean?" Dad said. The vein at the side of his forehead was sticking out.

She bent down and picked up Max's bottle, handed it to him, and settled him on her hip. "Of course I knew about it. I lent him the money for the fee, and I baby-sat Max."

Dad was shaking his head.

"I don't see the harm, Mitch. I think it's a good idea."

"Jean. You can't encourage . . ."

"Encourage what? A little optimism?"

"How's he going to go to college?" Dad spread out his left hand toward me. "How's he going to pay for tuition? And day care?"

"Mitch. He just took the test. He's not going anywhere. Yet." She smiled at me. "Right, Sam?"

I shrugged again. It was like they had all the words. No one had given me any.

Dad pointed at me. "We had an agreement, Sam. We had a deal. I'd pay for everything this year while you finished high school. But then you'd go work for Jeff Lawson." His finger swung toward Aunt Jean. "A good job. Steady work. He can pay for day care. He can pay me room and board. If he works hard, he'll make enough to get his own apartment."

Aunt Jean cocked her head at me. "Is that what you want, Sam? Work for Jeff Lawson? Work construction?" She nodded her head toward the math papers, the open book, the calculator. "Will you be happy doing that?"

Still no words. I shrugged again.

"Being happy doesn't have anything to do with it. It's not like he has a choice here, Jean," Dad said, his voice flat. "He already made his choice."

She whipped around so fast, Max's head wobbled. She put her free hand up to steady it. "You can't punish him for the rest of his life, Mitch Pettigrew. You should be proud of him."

They were talking about me like I wasn't even there.

"Mitch." Aunt Jean said, "it doesn't all have to be bad."

Dad snorted. "And where's the money coming from? Are you going to pay for college and child care, Jean? You and Ted?"

Aunt Jean pushed her head against Max's, her gray hair mixing with his soft blonde curls. He reached up and patted her face. "We can maybe help a little," she said.

"Nobody has to help. . . ," I started.

"You know this is what Theresa wanted, Mitch," Aunt Jean said.

Dad jerked, like something had stung him. He closed his eyes, once, a long, slow blink. "There's lots of things Theresa didn't know about."

"But I know what she wanted, Mitch. She wanted Sam to go to college. And if she were here, I know what she'd do."

They both just stared at each other. Dad fingering his beer bottle, Aunt Jean clutching Max.

Abruptly, Dad stood up. "If Theresa were here," he said, "we wouldn't be in this mess in the first place." He walked out of the room.

Aunt Jean sighed. Her eyes were thick with tears. She kissed Max on the forehead.

I stood up. I thought maybe I should hug her or something. But I just stood there. "It's okay, Aunt Jean. We're okay."

Her face crumpled a little. "I have to get home, Sam. I told Ted I'd just be a few minutes." She took a deep breath and nodded toward the bags, still sitting near the door. "You can freeze those or put them in the fridge. I taped instructions to all of them. Oh. And there's a couple of shirts and some pants I found for Max. At Target." She turned her head and gave Max another kiss, a loud smacking one this time. "Bye-bye, pumpkin." She handed him to me. Then she leaned over and kissed me, too, on the forehead, not so loudly. "You don't worry," she said. "You just take care of yourself and this baby."

When she was gone, I stood in the middle of the kitchen. I could put the food away. Or I could look at my SATs.

Max stirred in my arms and whimpered. I realized there was a warm wet stain on my chest.

First I'd change Max's diaper. As I walked past the table, I picked up the College Board envelope and tossed it into the garbage.

chapter eighteen

IT'S REALLY EARLY SATURDAY morning. I'm eight years old. I'm lying in bed, waiting.

The door to my room opens, slowly, and Dad pokes his head inside. "Sam," he whispers, "Sam, Sam, Sam."

I lie there, pretending to be asleep.

"Time to go fishing," Dad whispers.

"I'm already ready!" I shout, and I jump out of bed. And I am ready. I'd gotten back into bed with all my clothes on.

Dad laughs, like this is a really good joke, like he's never seen it before.

Mom is in the kitchen, making pancakes. She always makes pancakes before we go fishing. She's wearing jeans and a sweater and a pair of Dad's big woolly socks.

MARGARET BECHARD

"Clown feet," I say.

She grins at me. "Did you trick him again?"

"Yep." I sit at the table and pour lots of syrup on my pancakes.

While Mom and I do the dishes, Dad loads the truck with our gear. I climb up on the seat and sit in the middle. The truck smells funny, like wet dog, even though we don't have a dog. The seats are high, and my legs swing back and forth.

"This truck is way better than Andy's minivan," I say.

Dad's looking over his shoulder, backing down the driveway. "When you're sixteen, this can be your truck. I'll be ready for a new one about then." He glances at Mom, but she's looking out the window, smiling.

"Really? It can be my truck?" And I think about how cool that will be. "Me and Andy can go fishing together," I say.

Mom sighs. "I don't want to think about you and Andy driving around in this truck." She puts her arm around me and snuggles me against her. "Keep me warm until the heat kicks on."

We're going to one of Dad's secret spots. "Every fisherman needs to have a secret spot," he says to Mom, and she laughs. They talk over my head until Mom falls asleep. I try to sit still, so I won't wake her up. Dad turns the radio on, real quiet.

There are no other cars at Dad's secret spot. No people. Just the river and lots of rocks and lots of trees. The sun is behind thick clouds, and it's gloomy and cold.

"At least it's not raining," Dad says as he hands me my waders. He gave waders to Mom and me for Christmas. I sit down on a rock and pull mine on. They're big and heavy and clunky. They make me walk like Frankenstein.

They spend a long time setting up the rods, picking the right lines, the right flies. Dad's humming a little, under his breath. Mom shows me her collection of flies. I run my finger gently over them. "I think a redwing blackbird, don't you?" she asks. "Too bright," Dad says, but she just smiles and ties it on her line. She puts one on mine, too.

"I think I'll stay with Sam for a while," Mom says. "Help him practice."

Dad looks at her from under the brim of his lucky fishing hat. He's frowning. "Are you all right? You're not feeling sick again, are you?"

"I'm fine. I'm just . . . I don't feel like wading out too

far in that cold water." She gives a big exaggerated shiver, and I laugh because I know she wants me to. Because I know she doesn't want to talk about the medicine that makes her feel bad.

"Okay then," Dad says. "We can trade later." He wades out into the river, his rod high in his hand. When he finds a good place, he stands and flips the line back and forth over his head, then casts it out so the fly lands, gently, softly, in a smooth little pool behind the rapids.

I've only had my rod for a few months. I keep getting my line tangled, and, when I do make a cast, it doesn't sail out smooth and fast like Dad's. But Mom says "Good job," even when I get caught in a fallen tree branch.

When she's unfastened my snag, she says, "I think that's enough for one day," and I say, "Me too." She helps me pile rocks along the river's edge, to make a little bay. We sail twig boats back and forth.

Suddenly, Dad says, "Whoa, baby!" And then, "What a grab. Look at him go!"

Mom and I stand up and watch. His line is stretching out straight into the current. The rod is bent almost double. Dad is grinning, leaning back against the tension.

He works the fish back and forth, letting it run, then pulling it back toward him, maneuvering it around rocks where it tries to hide.

Finally, he's holding the pole high, reaching down into the water close by his leg. He looks over at us. "Come see, Sam. Wade out here."

"Isn't it too deep?" I look at Mom.

"It's fine, buddy," Dad says. "Really. It'll only be a little above your knees."

"Go on," Mom says. "It's not too deep."

I step out past my rock bay. The waders are insulated, but I can feel how cold the water is, right through them. I hold out my arms to keep my balance. Rocks roll and bump under my feet.

I look back at Mom. "Doing great," she says.

When I get to Dad, the water is past my knees. It's faster here, and I can feel it push against me.

Dad's got the rod tucked under his arm, and he's bent down, holding the fish close to his legs. He stretches out his free hand to me, and I stumble close up against him, pressing against his side. He shoves me gently around in front of him, so I'm between his legs. He's blocking the flow of the water, and I lean back against him. He feels as big and solid as one of the huge old Doug firs grow-ing along the shore.

He lifts the fish up a little, out of the water. It's big. As long as my arm. Its scales are a dull silver, and there's a red streak down its sides. "Isn't he a beaut?" Dad asks. He reaches around and opens the fish's mouth. He gently removes the barbless hook, caught in the jaw.

The fish is still and limp. "Is it dead?"

"No. Just worn out. He's strong. He put up quite a fight." Dad reaches down again, putting the fish back in the water. "Help me out here, Sam. Put one hand under his tail. Here." He slides my hand into place with his elbow. "And one under his belly."

I put my hands where he tells me, down in the water, under the fish. The water is really cold on my bare hands. Dad has his arms around me, holding the fish, too. I'm enclosed by him and the fish. "Hold him now," Dad whispers.

The fish is heavy and rough against my hands. In the water, the silver scales aren't dull. They wink and glis-ten. The tail fans, very slowly, and I feel its motion all through the fish's body.

"Keep the gills under the water," Dad says. "Watch

them work." His voice is soft and warm in my left ear.

I watch the gills bellow in and out, in and out.

We stand there in the river, Dad's arms wrapped around me. I'm not cold anymore. I can see the fish's eyes, bright and unblinking. I can feel him start to wiggle, feel him wanting to swim away, out of my hands. I tighten my grip.

The tail fans, harder, and the fish surges in my hands.

"Feel it?" Dad whispers, and I nod. The fish surges again.

I look over Dad's arm at Mom, standing on the shore, watching us, smiling. I want to say something to her, but I don't know what.

"Okay," Dad says, "he's ready to go. You did good, Fish." His hands open.

"Wait," I say. "Wait." And I stand there a minute longer, my hands around the fish, Dad's arms around me.

"Let him go now, Sam," he whispers. "Let him go."

I open my hands. There's a flash of silver and red, and the fish is gone.

chapter **nineteen**

DAD AND I ATE Aunt Jean's chili later that night. We didn't talk. Even Max was quiet, not banging on his tray or making blubby noises with his smushed peas.

"I'll do the dishes," I said, when Dad had scraped the last bean out of the dish.

"You cooked," he said, not looking up.

"I nuked it in the microwave, Dad. Big whup." I carried the empty dish and my bowl to the sink and ran the water. "Dad," I said. "I'm sorry I'm driving you crazy. I'm sorry I make you so mad. I'm sorry I've disappointed you. I'm sorry I took the SATs. It was a joke, mostly." I watched the water fill the dish and overflow down the drain.

"What Jean said . . ." Dad's voice was soft. "About

punishing you for the rest of your life? That isn't true."

"I know that." I shut the faucet off and turned to face him.

"If your mother . . ." He stopped, cleared his throat. "I've always known this was my fault, too, Sam." He looked sad and tired and old. He rubbed his hands over his face, and the look was gone.

Max laughed. He rubbed his hands on his face and grinned at Dad.

"I *am* proud of you, Sam," Dad said. I could barely hear him over Max's laughter.

"I know that," I said again, although I didn't know that. And I wanted to tell him that I didn't think it was his fault. None of this was his fault.

He kept looking at Max. "We do have to face reality."

"I know that, too." Which I did know. I knew all about reality.

Dad stood up. "I was up early. I'm going to bed."

"Okay," I said. "We'll try to keep it down."

He looked at me, for the first time since we'd started talking, and, for a second, I thought he was going to say something else. But he just turned and went out of the kitchen.

Only we didn't keep it down. Max didn't want to go to sleep. And then he didn't want to play or drink his bottle or even sit in the bathtub again. After about 11:30, all he wanted to do was cry.

Finally I carried him out into the living room, away from Dad's room. I tried to turn the TV on, but that seemed to just make him cry louder. So I turned out all the lights, and I lay down on the couch, with Max on my chest, still screaming.

I patted Max's back and started humming. A song Dad used to sing in the truck. Something about a raccoon and a Bible. I couldn't remember the words. All I could do was hum.

I thought about Brittany sitting on the couch in her living room. Brittany saying that she wasn't who she'd thought she'd be.

I could feel Max's face, hot and wet, through my T-shirt. And then I could feel his fists opening and then his whole body relaxing against mine. The cries turned to whimpers, then faded away.

I lay there, staring up at the ceiling. And I saw little bits of light. The glow-in-the-dark stars Mom had stuck on the ceiling for my sixth birthday party. I closed my eyes.

On Monday morning I was walking to Parenting, when Mrs. Harriman stepped out of her office. "Sam!"

I ran quick through my head—I'd handed in the Econ assignment on time. The government worksheets were late, but Mr. Walker didn't care. Ms. Garcia was probably disappointed and Mr. Gott was always mad. But Mrs. Harriman was smiling.

I crossed the hall. "Yeah?"

She held out her hand. "Congratulations!"

"What?"

Now she was totally smiling, the whole big-teeth thing. "Those SAT scores! 740 on the math! Way to go, Sam!"

I nearly said, "No kidding!" But I just shook her hand, instead.

"1320 total. That's very good, Sam." She still had hold of my hand. "Listen. I want you to come in and see me some time this week. We need to talk."

I wiggled my hand loose. "Okay. Sure. I'll do that." I went down the hall and around the corner, and then I just stood for a couple of minutes, leaning against the lockers. 740 on the math. Way better than I'd expected. Especially when Ms. Garcia's math thing was going so bad, making me feel like such a retard. I looked up and down the hall, wishing I'd see someone I knew, someone I could tell.

The phone rang early that night. 8:00. I thought it was going to be Claire, calling about her SATs. But it was Andy.

"What's up?" I was sitting in the living room. Max was hanging onto the coffee table, going around and around it.

"Hey," Andy said. "What's up with you?"

"Not much with me," I said.

"Not much with me, either," he said, and he laughed his maniac laugh. It was like fifth grade again. I put my feet up on the coffee table.

"Listen, man. It was cool on Saturday. Seeing you and Claire."

"Yeah. It was . . . good."

I could hear Andy fiddling with something. "The reason I'm calling," he said, "is my parents are going out of town this weekend, and Jenny's . . ." Whatever he was playing with clunked against the phone. "Sleeping over."

"Sleeping over?" It did sound like fifth grade, except not fifth grade, either.

"You know what I mean," Andy said. "Look. Jenny wants to have you and Claire come over for dinner. Saturday night."

"What?" I said.

"Dinner. Saturday night," he said again.

Max had worked his way around to where my legs blocked his path. He looked at me, then leaned over and drooled on my pants leg. I put my legs down. "Why would you want to have . . . I mean . . . if you have the place to yourself . . ."

"I know, I know." Andy sighed. "The thing is, Jenny wants to make dinner for people. She wants to ask Dan Jacobs and Melissa Talbot, too, but I said I had to ask you first because no way am I having dinner alone with Dan and Melissa. You remember Dan Jacobs?"

Of course I remembered Dan. I didn't have brain damage. I just had a kid. "He and Melissa are still together?"

"They are this month. Jeez. Let me tell you, you are lucky you've missed the whole Dan and Melissa Show."

And why wasn't Melissa pregnant? Better condoms? Dan and Melissa deserved to be pregnant. And then I felt bad for thinking that.

"Come on, Sam," Andy said. "You have to help me out here."

"The thing is, Andy, it's not like I can get a baby-sitter." Max had plopped down on his butt and was leaning over, trying to suck on his foot.

"No, no," Andy said. "That's the other thing. Jenny said you should bring Max. And Claire should bring, you know, Whosis."

"Emily."

"Right. We talked about this, Jenny and me. Bring the babies."

"Well, I don't know. I'll have to talk to Claire . . ."

"So then call me back, okay? You still know my number?"

I sighed. "Yes, Andy. I still know your number."

After I hung up, I realized I didn't know Claire's number. I was expecting her to call me, though. She hadn't called Saturday or Sunday. She'd definitely call tonight.

Max fell asleep at 9:30. I still had the government worksheets, and I was supposed to read *The Scarlet Letter* and I had math. I sat at my desk, staring at the chart I'd made, to remind me of all the stuff I needed to do for Max. I hadn't written anything on it in a long time.

By 10:00 she still hadn't called.

And not by 10:45.

Maybe she didn't want to talk to me. Maybe I'd made her mad. Said something. Done something. Not done something.

Maybe she had someone else she was talking to.

Get a grip, Sam, I thought. And I remembered that whole thing in the Taco Bell at the mall. Telling that woman that we were a family. Letting her believe that Emily was mine. It might be better if Claire didn't call. If we cooled it. Just a little bit.

By 11:05 I was positive she had someone she wanted to talk to more than me. I felt really rotten for the next seven and a half minutes.

"Hi," she said. "Sorry it's so late."

"That's okay," I said, "no problem." And quick, before I could change my mind, I said, "There's this thing. Saturday night."

"A thing?"

"At Andy's house."

"A thing at Andy's house?"

"He wants us to come. All of us. I mean, Emily and Max, too."

"Okay." She drew the word out long and slow. "I need just a few more clues here, Sam."

"Sorry." I took a breath. "Andy and Jenny are asking people over to Andy's house on Saturday night because his parents aren't home. For dinner."

"Aha." Claire laughed. "This sounds like Jenny."

"It does?"

"In ninth grade, she'd read Martha Stewart and clip recipes out of the newspaper. Her mom's like that, too, I guess. Maybe it's genetic."

"I don't know about that," I said. "Melissa Talbot and Dan Jacobs will be there, too. Do you . . . did you know them?"

"I knew Melissa." She made a little humming, Claire-thinking noise. "Well, I think we should go."

"You do?"

"Sure. I think it sounds like fun."

"Fun?"

She laughed. "Yes, Sam. Going out. Meeting people. Talking. Eating together. It sounds like fun. Don't you think so?"

"Well . . . I guess," I said.

"Oh," Claire said, "by the way. Did you get your SAT scores?"

"I . . . yeah."

"I got 1340." Her voice was a little hesitant, like she was happy but not sure I'd be.

"I got 1320."

"Sam! Good job! What was your math?"

"740."

"Wow. My verbal was 750." She sighed. "Doomed to be an English major. Gemma got 1400."

"Wow."

"Yeah. You wish you could hate that girl, but she's just too dang nice."

"Right."

"So. Anyway, call Andy and tell him we'll come. You and me and the kids."

"Right," I said. "You and me and the kids."

chapter twenty

I PICKED EMILY AND Claire up on Saturday night. I wanted to drive to Andy's. Claire was wearing a pair of low black jeans and a pair of shoes with big soles that made her about four inches taller. She had on a tight blue top that showed her bellybutton.

She grinned at the look on my face. "Do I look okay?"

"Oh. Yeah. You look . . . you look great."

She grinned wider. "My mother says nursing mothers shouldn't wear tops like this."

"Looks okay to me." And I was glad I'd put on a clean white T-shirt and the jeans without the holes in the butt.

We stowed Emily and her car seat and the diaper bag and Claire's purse and a folding crib into the back of the

Datsun with Max. Max tried to grab Emily, but the straps on his car seat were too tight. He gave me a shriek.

Claire settled into the front seat. "The crib's in case one of them falls asleep," she said. "Keep your fingers crossed."

I backed carefully down the driveway. "Did your mom say anything? I mean, about us going out?"

Claire shook her head, rattling her earrings. Then she frowned. "Why? Did your dad say something?"

I'd told him where I was going. I'd told him I was going with Claire. He'd just given me his look. A disappointed-in-Sam look. No more I'm-proud-of-you-Sam stuff. "He didn't say anything."

Behind me, Max gave another shriek. I jerked around. He was pulling at the car seat straps. When he saw me looking, he shrieked again. "Jeez, Max," I said. "Cool it."

My voice was maybe a little loud, because Claire raised her eyebrows at me. "Take it easy, Sam. He's just excited."

I shook my head. "That screaming just . . . it drives me crazy." I slowed for the turn to Andy's street.

"He's asserting his independence," Claire said. "Didn't

you read Chapter Twelve in the parenting book?"

I hadn't read the parenting book in three weeks. If I did the English reading, I couldn't read anything else. Not that I was doing the English reading. "The parenting book drives me crazy, too." I didn't understand how they could expect anybody to do even half the stuff in that book. Or even remember it.

Claire put her hand on my leg. "You seem kind of tense. Is it tonight?"

I shook my head. "No."

Her hand tightened, gently. "You know, Sam. Sometimes I wish you could tell me more what you're thinking."

I looked at her, her face lit by the lights from the dash. And I realized how much I wished that, too. "I've got a lot of homework piling up," I said, finally.

"I could help you with English. And you could help me with math." She put her hand on my arm. "See. Together we almost make one complete person."

I didn't know what to say.

I pulled into Andy's driveway. Andy and Jenny came out the front door, like they'd been waiting for us. Jenny took Max from me as soon as I had him out of the car seat. "Come with Aunt Jenny," she said, and she and Claire hustled both babies into the house.

I tossed Andy the diaper bag and Claire's purse and my backpack. I got the portable crib. "Holy hannah," Andy said, "this stuff is heavier than my football gear."

I hadn't heard anybody say "holy hannah" in a long time. Mostly because only Andy ever said it. I laughed, and I felt a little better.

Andy's house was exactly the way I remembered, and that made me feel better, too. Like I hadn't missed anything. Jenny and Claire stopped in the kitchen. Two girls were sitting at the kitchen table, drinking cans of Coors. "Sam, Claire. This is Melissa and Renee."

"Hi, Sam," Melissa said. "It's been a long time."

I nodded. Renee gave me a little wave. She had thick curly dark hair and a nose ring. I didn't know her at all. I figured she might be just a little drunk.

Claire sat down, Emily on her lap. I pointed to Andy's load. "Where do you want this stuff?"

"I'll need the diaper bag and my purse. I guess, just lean the crib against the wall there. Till we need it."

"Okay." I knew they were all watching us, Melissa

and Renee and Jenny and Andy. I put the crib down and held my hands out toward Max. "I'll take him."

"Oh, no." Jenny turned sideways. "You go in the family room with the other guys." She waved her free hand at me. "Really. We'll be fine."

Dan was sitting on the couch facing the TV. There was a guy next to him I didn't know.

"Sam," Andy said, "this is Brandon. He's on the football team, too."

Brandon stood up and held his hand out over the coffee table. "Brandon," he said. He was as tall as me, but a lot heavier.

"Sam," I said. We shook, and he sat back down.

On the TV, Bruce Willis was lying on the floor under a table, shooting a guy who was standing on top of the table. Machine-gun fire burst around me, echoing around the room.

"Surround sound!" Andy said. "We just got it!"

"Cool!" The TV was new, too. Bigger.

Andy sat in the chair to the left of the couch. He pointed to the recliner just beyond him. "Your chair, Pettigrew," he said.

I crossed over and sat down, listening to the familiar creak of the leather. I'd always sat here when I came over to Andy's.

"This sucks on commercial television," Brandon said. "They're cutting out all the good parts."

"You want a beer, Sam?" Andy asked. There were three on the table, half empty, and a bag of chips. "They're in the fridge."

"I . . ." I didn't want to drink if I was driving the babies home. "I'm good for now." I took a breath. I was, just a little, panicked. Because I realized this was the first time, the first time in a long time, I'd been around just a group of guys. Except once, in the parking lot at school, when I'd stood around for a couple of minutes with Michael and a few of the boyfriends. And even then, we'd talked about babies.

Brandon picked up the clicker and started switching channels. A Victoria's Secret commercial flashed on. "Stop!" Dan, Andy, and I all shouted at once. We watched the whole commercial in complete silence.

"Those are the best commercials on TV," Dan said.

"No kidding," I said. And I settled back in the chair a little.

Andy took a swig of his beer. "I got my SAT scores." He shook his head. "1240. Pretty weak."

"I got 980," Brandon said. "Last time I got 950. I figure, if they let me take it, like twenty more times, I'll get a decent score."

"Of course, you'll be forty years old," Dan said, and Brandon punched him, pretty hard. "I got a 1280. 640 verbal, 640 math."

"Woo-hoo," Brandon said. "Aren't we special." He'd clicked back to *Die Hard*. "Watch this," he said. "I love this part."

And then, I don't know why, but I said, "I got 740 on the math. 1320 total."

They all looked at me. Dan had his beer bottle halfway to his mouth.

"Whoa. Sam. Way to go." Andy stuck out his hand so I could slap it.

"You could get into a good college. Score like that," Dan said.

"Yeah, well, I'll get into Oregon State," Brandon said. "That's all I care about." He stood up. "I'm getting another beer," and he wandered off toward the kitchen.

Dan shook his head. "I'm going out of state. I don't

want to hang around Oregon any longer than I have to. My brother goes to school in California. He says the girls wear bikinis every day."

Andy and I both laughed. "I'm sure that's a reason to pick a college," Andy said.

Dan drained his beer. "They have a good engineering program, too. Hey, Brandon!" he shouted. "Bring me another one!"

Andy looked at me. "Remember how we talked about going to Georgetown?"

I nodded. "Because we liked the Hoyas."

Andy grinned. "Not that I could get into Georgetown."

"Yeah," I said. "I'm not planning on it either."

Brandon came back with the two beers. "The kitchen," he said, "is full of babies." He handed a beer to Dan.

"That's right." Dan took a sip of the Coors. "How's that going? The baby thing?"

"It's okay."

"One of them's yours?" Brandon asked.

I nodded.

He took a big swig of beer. "That must suck," he said.

"Brandon," Andy said. "Shut up."

Renee and Melissa walked in. Renee linked her arm

through Brandon's. "Dinner's gonna be like a long time, and we're bored. You guys want to come outside and play basketball?"

Dan peered out the window. "Isn't it raining?"

Melissa made a face. "Omigod," she said. "You're such a wuss, Daniel."

"It stopped raining a little while ago," Renee said.

Andy stood up. "It's not like we don't know how the movie ends, guys."

"Everything's going to be wet," Dan said. But he finished his beer and stood up.

I stopped off in the kitchen. Jenny was doing something with lettuce. Claire was feeding Emily, a blanket draped over her. Max was sitting in the middle of the floor surrounded by pots and pans. He was banging a spoon on the lid of one of the pots. He didn't even look up at me.

"Are you going outside, too?" Jenny asked. She sounded a little ticked, like maybe this wasn't part of her dinner plan.

"I guess . . . " I pointed toward the door. "Renee and Melissa want to shoot baskets." I looked at Claire. "Do you want to . . . I mean, when Emily's done? I could hold her or something."

Claire smiled up at me. "That's okay. It's pretty wet outside."

"That's what Dan keeps saying." I could hear the sound of the basketball smacking the pavement. "It's probably cold, too."

Claire nodded, still smiling. Jenny was ripping lettuce. Max pounded the pan.

I didn't know what I was supposed to do. I felt kind of bad, leaving Claire there. And I couldn't tell if she wanted me to stay inside.

But I didn't want to stay inside.

Andy stuck his head around the dining room door. "Hey, Sam. We need you to move your car."

"Okay," I said. I looked at Claire. "I'll be right back."

Claire nodded. She and Jenny exchanged a look.

I put the Datsun out on the street. As I was walking back up the driveway, Andy threw me the ball. "Think fast, Pettigrew!" he shouted.

It was sort of a basketball free-for-all, after that. Everybody just kind of grabbing for the ball. Lots of pushing and shoving and not very much shooting. After about ten minutes, Brandon and Renee started playing mostly with each other, grabbing and tickling until Brandon carried her off around the side of the garage. Then Melissa got hit in the back of the head, and she went and sat on the steps, huddled up. Dan shrugged and went and sat beside her. They started arguing, softly.

So then it was just Andy and me.

Neither one of us had put on a jacket, and it was cold. I could see my breath as I bent over, panting, waiting to try to knock the ball out of his hands. He tried to power around me, and I shoved into him, hard, grabbing for the ball, trying to slap it loose. Both of us trash talking. He spun away from me, slipped and landed on his butt. We laughed so hard, we couldn't talk.

I grabbed the ball while he was still down. "Hey!" he shouted and jumped up. I was rusty, and he stole it right back. He dribbled past and made a shot. The ball clanged off the backboard and bounced back into the driveway. We both chased after it before it could roll out into the street.

"It's mine," I panted, jostling Andy.

"No way!" Andy shouted. "Hands off!" He bumped me, hard, with his shoulder. My feet slipped on the wet pavement, and I sprawled into the grass at the side of the driveway. It knocked the breath out of me, and I lay there for a minute, thinking how much I'd missed this. How much I'd missed just running as fast as I could and taking some hits. Messing around.

I flipped over on my back, watching my little clouds of breath, my fingers and ears stinging with the cold, my back soaked from the wet grass. And I wished I could always be here, on Andy's driveway, with nothing else to think about but the next basket. Who was going to get the next shot. Keeping the ball out of the street.

Andy leaned over me. "You okay, man?"

I closed my eyes.

The door opened behind us. "Dinner's ready," Jenny said.

I realized I was hungry, but I didn't want to get up. I didn't want to go in the house. I just wanted to lie here in the wet grass.

"Sam?" Andy said.

I kept my eyes closed. "Did you know NASA sent a probe to Jupiter, and the pressure crushed it to bits in 57.6 minutes?"

"You're freakin' me out here, man," Andy said.

I opened my eyes. "Sometimes I freak myself out."

MARGARET BECHARD

chapter twenty-one

ANDY BALANCED THE BALL, carefully, on my forehead.
"You know, you're probably lying in dog . . ."

I pushed myself up onto my hands. I could hear
Brandon and Renee, laughing as they went up the steps.

The door banged open. "Sam!" It was Claire, her
voice shrill and panicky. "Sam! Come quick!"

I moved so fast, I nearly knocked Andy sprawling. I
took the steps in one jump and pushed past Brandon and
Renee. Claire was standing just inside the door, clutching Emily. "It's Max. He's bleeding . . ."

I ran back to the kitchen.

Jenny was holding Max. There was blood all over.
Streaks on the floor. Streaks on Max. On his face, his
clothes, his legs. He was screaming at the top of his lungs.

There was blood on Jenny, too. And she was crying louder than Max. He was flailing at her, smacking her with his hands. More blood was flying into her face.

"What happened? What happened?" Glass crunched under my feet as I crossed to them and snatched Max out of Jenny's arms. I tried to cradle him, tried to see where all the blood was coming from, but he thrashed and wiggled in my arms.

"I broke some wineglasses. They slipped." Jenny was sobbing. "And he's so quick. You never told me he was so quick!"

My fault, my fault. My responsibility.

Max twisted in my arms, screaming. There was blood on my hands, on my shirt. "But where . . ." I couldn't seem to get my breath, and my heart was beating so hard it hurt. "I can't see . . ."

"It's his hand, Sam." Andy reached over my arm, and he grabbed Max's right hand, forced it open. "See. It's his hand."

A broad cut crossed Max's palm. Blood ran bright and red down his hand and his wrist. Andy whistled. "That's going to need stitches." He reached behind him and grabbed a washcloth out of a drawer. "Hold this tight."

I pinned Max with my left arm and held the cloth as hard as I could against the cut. Max struggled, but I was too strong for him to pull free. Tears and snot and drool all ran down his face, onto my arm.

"Maybe we should call an ambulance," Claire said. She was standing just in the doorway, Emily silent and big-eyed in her arms. Brandon and Renee hovered behind her, their faces white in the dark dining room.

"No," I said. I couldn't wait there, with the blood and the crying. I had to get moving. I had to do something. "I'll drive him to the emergency room."

"I'll drive," Andy said. He jiggled his car keys. "You'll need to hold that cloth on him."

Clutching Max to my chest, I followed Andy out to the garage. I thought Claire said something, but I didn't stop to listen.

Andy drove fast. He'd always been a good driver. "Straight shot up 217 to St. Vincent's," he said as we got on the on-ramp. "Be there in ten minutes. Seven maybe."

I nodded. Max was still crying, but he'd stopped wiggling and twisting.

"God," Andy said. "There was blood all over." He glanced at me. "It's just his hand, Sam. Really. I mean, it's just a cut on his hand. No big deal." He put his hand on Max's head. "Your first stitches, big guy. Welcome to the club."

I took a deep breath. Max took a deep breath, too, sobby and gaspy. The adrenaline had stopped zinging through me, although I could taste it, sharp and metallic. I felt exhausted and sick. "You'll be okay, Max," I said.

He started to cry again.

Andy found a parking place right next to the emergency room. Max was still crying as we rushed through the big glass doors. He was hoarse, he'd been crying so long.

A woman was sitting behind a counter with a computer monitor. As I carried Max toward her, a nurse came through a pair of swinging doors to the left. "What happened?" She grabbed Max from me, and he screamed even louder. "What happened?" she yelled again, over Max.

And I realized I didn't know exactly what had happened.

"He cut his hand," Andy said. "A glass broke, and he was on the floor . . ."

MARGARET BECHARD

"Are you his brother?" She was talking to Andy. "We need his parents."

"I'm his parent," I said. "I'm his father."

She nodded. "It's okay, baby," she said to Max. She looked at me. "What's his name?"

"Max," Andy and I said together.

She carried him off through the swinging doors.

"Wait . . . ," I said.

The first woman leaned out from behind the counter. "I need to get some information."

When we were done, she said, "We'll bill your insurance."

I nodded. "Can I go back there now? With him?"

She smiled. "You just make yourself comfortable in the waiting area. Someone will be out to see you soon."

I looked around the waiting room. It was like a giant living room, with chairs and sofas and little tables with lamps. There was a guy sitting in the corner by the window. He looked like he was asleep. Otherwise the place was empty.

I sat down on the couch closest to the swinging doors. Andy sat down next to me. Then he bounced back up. "I'm going to find a phone. Let them know we got here okay." He walked off across the room and disappeared down a hallway.

I leaned my head back on the couch. My stomach growled. My hands and arms were sticky with blood.

The outside doors whooshed open, and a woman and a kid came in. The kid was cradling his left arm in his right, pressing it against his body. Both of them looked at me and then looked away.

A different nurse came out, and the woman said, "It's his wrist. I think it's broken." Her voice was loud and sharp, like she'd been holding these words in for a long time and had to let them out.

The nurse led the kid through the doors, and Counter Lady collected the mother.

Andy came back. He was laughing. "You're not going to believe this."

"What?"

"It turns out, most of that blood wasn't even Max's. It was Jenny's."

"Jenny's?"

"Yeah. In all the excitement, she didn't even notice. I guess she has a huge cut on the bottom of her foot. She didn't have shoes on, you know."

MARGARET BECHARD

"Is she coming here?" And I imagined Jenny coming in, covered in blood. They'd think . . . I didn't know what they'd think.

"Naw. They're going to Meridian Park. Her dad works there." Andy sat down and put his head in his hands. "It seemed so simple, you know. Have a few people over for dinner."

Across the room, Counter Lady was leading the woman through the swinging doors. How come she got to go in? Because she was a mother? If Max had a mother, would he have someone in there with him now?

". . . since Claire's there alone," Andy said.

I looked at him. "What?"

Andy sighed. "Melissa and Dan took off. Melissa can't stand blood or something stupid like that. So Brandon was going to drive Jenny to the hospital, and Renee wanted to go along. I don't know. There was something about Emily's car seat."

"It's in the Datsun," I said. "Locked in the Datsun. Probably Claire wouldn't take Emily without the car seat."

"Yeah. Well. And Claire thought you might call . . ."

"I will. When I know something definite."

"So I was thinking, dude. I'm not doing anything here . . ."

I sat up straight. "Look, Andy. You go home. Keep Claire and Emily company. I'll call when I need a ride." I looked over at the swinging doors. "It could be a long time."

"That's what I was thinking." Andy stood up. "But call. We'll come right away. No kidding."

"Thanks, Andy." I held out my hand, and we shook.

"You might want to go clean up a little, Sam," Andy said, wiping his hand on his pant leg.

When I came out of the bathroom, two guys had taken my couch. I sat in a chair in the corner. It was the first time in a long time that I'd been all by myself. I sat there, hunched forward, staring down at my clean hands. And I thought about Max and me and what had happened. I thought about Claire and Emily. And I thought how weird it was to think you absolutely knew something—to be so absolutely certain—and then to realize that you really didn't know anything at all.

After a long time, a new woman, in green scrubs, with a stethoscope around her neck, came through the swinging doors. She was holding a clipboard. She looked at me. "Mr. Pettigrew?"

I nearly said my dad wasn't there, but I stopped myself just in time. I nodded and stood up.

She held out her hand. "I'm Dr. Fisher."

She was even smaller than Ms. Garcia, and her hand felt tiny and fragile in mine. She had big dark circles under her eyes, and her hair was sticking up, like she'd slept on it funny. She looked about two years older than me.

"I took care of Max," she said.

I tried to swallow the lump in my throat, couldn't, so I just nodded again.

She held up her right hand. "The cut on his hand. Here . . ." And she ran her finger across the base of her thumb. "It was quite deep. And we had to put in a few stitches." She dropped her hand and, without warning, her face relaxed in a big warm smile. "He's just fine. It looked much worse than it was."

Suddenly, it was like my lungs were twice as big as usual. Air rushed inside of me.

"Would you like to see him?" she asked, still smiling.

"Yes," I said.

I followed her through the doors, down a narrow hallway, into a little examining room. A nurse was sitting in the corner. She was holding Max. He wasn't wearing anything but a diaper. A diaper and two big bandages, one on each hand. He was drinking out of a bottle.

"We got him some formula from peds," the nurse said. "For being such a brave boy."

"Both hands?" I asked the doctor.

She nodded. "There are some superficial cuts on his left hand. And we removed a few splinters of glass."

Max had shifted at the sound of my voice. Now he pushed away the bottle and held out his hands, silently.

I went over and picked him up. He wrapped his arms, tight around my neck and pressed his head against my shoulder. The fingers of his left hand twined gently into the curls on my neck.

And I held him against me, hanging on to him as tight as I could.

The doctor put her hand on his back. "So what exactly happened?"

I took a couple of deep breaths, and it felt like Max matched me, breath for breath. "He was on the floor in the kitchen. Playing with some pots and pans. And

Jenny dropped . . ." I nearly said "some wineglasses."
"Two glasses," I said. "They broke, and Max grabbed a piece."

The doctor was nodding, taking notes on the clipboard. "Jenny is his mother?"

"No. She's Andy's friend. We were at Andy's house." It seemed like so much to explain.

"Where is his mother?" the doctor asked.

I wanted to ask what difference that made. But I said, "Boise." The doctor and nurse exchanged a look around me, and I tightened my grip on Max. "I'm the custodial parent."

The doctor looked at her clipboard again. The circles under her eyes were darker, and her face looked thin and tight. "Well, Sam. It's Sam, isn't it?" I nodded. "You have to be very careful. You have to watch them every minute. Especially as they get more mobile."

I nodded. Max's fingers tightened, pulled on my hair. I did watch him. All the time. Almost every minute.

There were voices in the hall. A woman's voice, Counter Lady, then a man's. A voice I recognized.

"Here they are," Counter Lady said, and Dad walked in.

We all just stared at him. The doctor, the nurse, me, Max.

"Claire called me," he said. "She thought you might need . . . " His face twisted a little. "Something."

I knew he was probably mad. I knew he was probably really and truly pissed. But relief flooded over me, so strong, I nearly had to sit down.

But I didn't. I just clutched Max tighter. "We need a ride home," I said.

MARGARET BECHARD

chapter twenty-two

DAD HELD UP A plastic grocery bag. "I brought some spare clothes."

Max whimpered when I set him down on the examining table, but he let me dress him in the shirt and pants Dad had brought. They were the ones Aunt Jean had bought at Target. The tags were still on them.

The doctor talked to Dad, explaining how she'd stitched Max up. How she didn't think she needed to call social services. She kept smiling at Dad. He looked a little confused, like he still wasn't sure exactly what was going on.

When I had Max dressed, I picked him up again, and he wrapped his arms back around my neck. The doctor started explaining stuff about changing the bandages and putting antiseptic cream on. She kept saying, "Sam, you'll need to do this" and "Sam, you'll need to do that," but she kept looking over at Dad to make sure he was listening, make sure he was getting it all. So I just held on to Max.

Finally, she'd said everything she needed to say, and I signed something on the clipboard, and then Max and I followed Dad out into the parking lot.

The Datsun was parked under one of the lights near the door.

"How did you get it here?"

"She . . . Claire said it was at Andy's, locked up. She needed to get her car seat out, and she said you'd need Max's seat."

Dad opened the passenger door and flipped the seat forward so I could put Max in the back. "Ted gave me a ride over with the spare key. Your backpack is in there, too. She . . . Claire had it all packed and ready to go."

I thought Max might have a fit when I put him in the car seat, but he just sighed and leaned his head back, like he knew we were going home.

I climbed into the passenger seat, and I leaned back, too. I felt the way I had freshman year when I tried to run the mile under five minutes to impress the track coach. Drained and wobbly.

Max fell sound asleep in the car. I guess he was pretty wiped out, too. He didn't wake up when I carried him into the house, or when I put him in his crib, carefully, on his back. I stood there and looked at him, sprawled out, his bandaged hands up above his head. I pulled the blanket up over him, made sure the window was closed, left my desk light on, in case he woke up scared.

Dad came in and put his hand on my shoulder. I thought he was going to start in. Tell me how stupid I was. Irresponsible. But he said, "You look pretty wiped out."

I shook my head. "I can't believe I let it happen. I can't believe I was so stupid."

He patted my shoulder. "Get some sleep. You'll feel better in the morning."

"Yeah," I said. "Right."

I flopped down on the bed. It was too hard to take my clothes off. Dad tugged off my shoes. He pulled the blankets up over me. "Should I turn off the light?"

"No. Leave it on for Max."

"Okay. I'll leave it on for Max," he said.

I lay there, flat on my back, staring up at the ceiling. For some reason, I wondered about the kid with the broken wrist and his mother. I wondered if they were okay. And I wondered how I could do what I knew I had to do.

We didn't wake up until 8:05. I went out to the kitchen and heated up Max's bottle, and brought it back into the bedroom. I picked him up and got back into bed with him. I propped myself up on the headboard and fed him his bottle. It was like when he was really little, and I had to feed him in the middle of the night. He could have held the bottle himself now, in spite of the bandages, but he leaned back on my arm and sucked away dreamily, his eyes half closed. He reached up with his right hand, and I bent down a little so he could touch my face. "I do love you, Max," I whispered. "From that first day in the hospital. I've always loved you."

I carried him into the bathroom to change him and put new bandages on his hands. He didn't fight and squirm like usual, even when I put the cream on his cuts. I looked at myself in the mirror. I'd slept in my clothes. I had blood on my shirt. Jenny's or Max's. My hair was sticking to my forehead.

I sat Max in his crib with the stuffed bunny Aunt

Connie had sent. He sucked one of the bunny's ears into his mouth and started chewing on it.

I made the shower as hot as possible, and I just stood there, letting it wash over me, watching the soapy water pool around my feet.

When I was dressed, I carried Max into the kitchen. Dad was sitting at the table. There was a bowl of batter on the counter. "I thought I'd make pancakes. Does Max like pancakes?"

"I don't know."

It turned out Max loved pancakes. He sat in his high chair, and Dad fed him, little bits, gently, on the end of his fork. Dad talked in his goofy voice, and Max laughed, showing us the pancake mush in his mouth.

Dad glanced at me. "I can make some for you, too."

I hadn't eaten since lunch yesterday, but somehow I wasn't hungry. "Maybe later."

I sat there and watched him feed Max, and I tried to figure out how to find the words to say what I'd been thinking.

The doorbell rang.

"I'll get it," I said.

Claire was standing on the porch. "Hi!" she said. She

jogged up and down, her breath coming out in little cloudy puffs. She was wearing sweatpants and a hooded Nike sweatshirt. Her hair was pulled back in a ponytail high on her head. "I was going for my run, and I thought I'd check on you guys. I mean, Max is okay, right?"

"I—no. He's fine. Jeez, Claire." I shook my head. "I'm sorry. I should have called last night."

She stopped jogging. "I knew you'd call if anything really bad had happened. Can I see him?"

I stepped back. "Sure. Come on in."

She followed me to the kitchen. "It's Claire," I said.

Dad nodded.

Claire leaned over and patted Max's head. "Hey, there, big guy. You scared us half to death."

"He's got stitches in his right hand," I said, "but mostly it's just little cuts."

"He's fine," Dad said.

"Good," Claire said. "That's really good." She jammed her hands into her sweatshirt pocket. "I guess I should be going."

And I knew I'd have to tell her, too. "Dad. Would it be okay . . . could you watch Max for me? Just for a little while?" I nodded my head toward the door. "I want to walk up to the school with Claire. Just up to the school and back."

I looked at her. Claire was looking at me. Surprised, but happy. Relieved, maybe.

"Sure," Dad said. "We'll be okay." He wiped at Max's face with a napkin. Some of the paper stuck to his cheeks. "We'll be okay for a little while."

I got my jacket and followed Claire outside. She slipped her hand into mine as we went down the driveway. "I'm sorry I didn't call," I said.

She squeezed my hand. "I understand. I mean, it must have been pretty crazy."

I shook my head. It was the scariest thing that had ever happened to me.

"You should have seen it at Andy's house after you left. Once we got Jenny's sock off and saw, like, this huge gash, and Melissa just went berserk, and Jenny couldn't stop crying, and Brandon kept yelling at everybody to stay calm." Claire shook her head, and her ponytail swung against my shoulder.

"Is Jenny okay?"

"Yeah. She had to get stitches, too. The weird thing, though? I was cleaning up, after everybody had gone to the hospital. And, really, it was just those two little wineglasses that broke." She shook her head again. "By the look of that kitchen, you'd have thought we broke every friggin' glass in the house."

We walked in silence down Alder and along Sycamore and across the front lawn of the elementary school. We went around behind the gym to the playground.

I sat on one of the swings. Claire climbed partway up the climbing structure. "Did you go to school here?"

"Kindergarten through fifth." I grabbed the chains and leaned back. The sky was heavy with thick gray clouds. It was going to rain again.

"I went to Fir Grove. I remember, in first grade, I was terrified of the slide. I couldn't make myself go down it." She clomped to the top of the climbing structure, to the platform at the top of the slide. She slid down, fast, her arms up above her head. Then she walked over to the swings. She sat down on the one next to me and patted my leg. "What's wrong, Sam?"

I thought of all the times she'd asked me that. All the times she'd asked and I'd said, "Nothing." Or made something up.

"I think I'm going to give Max up for adoption."

chapter twenty-three

HER HAND TIGHTENED ON my leg. "Sam?" She leaned down, trying to peer closer at my face. "Sam. What are you talking about?"

I sat forward, my elbows on my knees, my hands dangling. "I can't do this anymore, Claire. And I can't do it to Max."

The chains creaked, and I could tell she was leaning back, away from me. "It's just some cuts on his hands, you know."

The wind picked up a little pile of leaves and blew them in a tight circle. "It's not just last night. It's not . . . it's all kinds of stuff." I looked at her. "Stuff I've been thinking about for a long time."

She was frowning the way she did when she was trying

hard to figure something out, like a word analogy or a geometry problem. "Is it about wanting to go to college?"

"No," I said. "No. It's not about college." And, in a way, I thought, in a way, it had more to do with playing basketball with Andy. But I couldn't tell her that.

"Because, I mean, you don't have to . . ." She was leaning forward again, her hands clasped tight on her knees. "I mean, you had this plan, right? The construction job? You don't have . . . Nothing's changed."

I shook my head. No. Nothing had changed.

"I thought you knew . . . that day in the library, you told me you knew what you wanted." Her voice was tight, high. Like she was trying not to cry.

"I thought I did, Claire. I really, really thought I did know."

"Look." She stood up so suddenly her swing banged into my legs. She moved over in front of me, gripping the chains above my head. "You had a bad night, Sam. I mean, there's no question about that. And I can totally understand how . . . but, the thing is, you should at least talk to Mrs. Harriman. There are people who can help you. There are people who would love to help you. If you just try."

"Claire." I reached up and put my hands over hers. I had to lean back, like I was about to start swinging, pump myself up real high. "I have been trying. I've been trying my best."

She closed her eyes, then opened them, and they were filling with tears. She gave the chains one hard shake, then pulled her hands loose from under mine. She turned around and started walking away. And I didn't know if I should stop her, follow her. I jammed my hands deep into the pockets of my jacket.

She stopped next to the slide and turned her head. "I can't believe you're just giving up, Sam."

My hands clenched. "Claire. Honest to God. Don't you think it's better for a kid to have a real father?" I squinted across the playground. The wind was piling the leaves up against the wall of the gym. "Don't you think everybody ought to have a mother?"

"You must think I'm terrible." Her voice was thick with tears.

"I . . . what?"

"Because I'm keeping Emily."

I took a deep breath, and the air was cold in my mouth, in my chest. "I don't think you're terrible, Claire. I don't think Gemma's terrible. Or Nicole. Or anybody. I think you're all amazing. But I can't do what you're doing. It's not the same for me."

"But it is. I can tell it is. I know you love Max. I know you can make this work, Sam."

"I do love Max. I love him . . ." I closed my eyes for a second, then opened them. "But I think he deserves more. He shouldn't just be something that somebody has to make work."

She didn't say anything. She bent her head away from me, and I could tell she was crying. I sat there and watched the leaves blow around.

"I liked you, Sam," she said, quietly, to the bark dust between her feet. "I liked you a lot."

"I know," I said. "I like you, too."

She looked at me. "There were things I've been thinking . . ."

"I know."

She tipped her head back and looked up at the clouds. Neither one of us said anything. Then she sighed. "It's going to rain. And I have to get home and feed Emily."

Her and Emily, her and Emily and me and no Max. I felt a stab, a hot, hard stab of pain.

We walked back to my house. We didn't hold hands. At the end of my driveway, we stopped. I thought she was going to say something. Argue with me some more. But she just gave me a funny, sad half-smile. Then she turned and walked, then ran down the sidewalk.

Dad was sitting in the living room, reading a fishing magazine. "Max got sleepy, so I put him in his crib. He's in there, kind of muttering to himself. We used to do that with you," he added.

"That's okay," I said. "He's fine like that." I crossed over to the TV.

"Did Claire go home?"

I nodded.

Dad frowned. "What's wrong? Did something happen, Sam?"

I picked up the clicker. Put it back down. "I've decided to give Max up for adoption." It wasn't any easier to say.

I looked at him. He'd been holding the magazine, but now he dropped it, with a loud slap, on the coffee table. "What? Just now? You decided this just now?"

I shook my head. "No. Not . . . I've been thinking about it." I didn't know exactly when I'd decided. "I've been thinking, you know, how you were right. All along."

And, suddenly, no warning, no pricking in the eyes, no tightening in the chest, suddenly, I burst into tears. Big, huge gulping sobs that got louder and sloppier the harder I tried to stop them.

I turned around and faced the window, trying to stop, trying to pull myself together.

Dad's chair scraped across the floor. And then he had his arms around me, and he turned me around to face him, and he pulled me tight against his shoulder and patted my back. Which made me cry harder, made my whole body shake with crying.

Finally, after a long time, I managed to step back. I took a deep, shuddery breath. "It's not what happened last night."

"I know," Dad said.

"And it's not that he's going to want stuff. Shoes and hockey and . . ." I couldn't think of all the things Max might want. I took another breath. "And it's not about me . . . going to college or . . . or getting married." I looked up at him, and his face was blurry. "But I could never get married. I could never have another kid."

"I know," Dad said.

I coughed and folded my arms across my chest. Get

a grip, Sam. Stop whining. "So, anyway, you know, I just . . . I thought . . ." I coughed again and tightened my arms. "Aunt Jean likes him so much."

"Ah," Dad said. "Right." He shifted his feet. "The thing is, Sam, back when . . ." He rubbed his hand across his chin. "Back when Max first came here, Jean and I talked quite a bit. And, well, Ted is fifty-eight, and Jean will be fifty-six in March."

I nodded. "I didn't know that."

He nodded, too. "It's just more than they . . . a baby and all . . ."

I nodded again. "I can understand that," I said, trying to keep my voice firm, level. I'd been thinking there might be an easy way. That maybe I could be like a favorite uncle. Uncle Sam. Disappointment and pain and fear arced through me.

"The thing is," Dad said. He picked up the clicker, put it back down. "There is an agency. Jean talked to the priest at her church. Back when you first found out. And he told her about this agency."

All I could do was nod, the ache closing my throat, choking my words.

Dad put his arms back around me.

The wind rattled the window. The furnace tick-ticked in the basement. Max fussed, just a little, in his crib. "Do you think I'm doing the right thing?" I said, softly.

Dad sighed. "Sam. I wish I knew what to tell you. All along, I've wished I knew what to tell you."

Max gave a yelp, and then a shriek. "I've got to get him," I said.

Max had pulled himself up and was standing, hanging onto the crib rail. "Bah!" he shouted when he saw me in the doorway. "Bah! Bah!"

"Bah! Bah!" I said back. I looked around the room, and I imagined no crib, no diaper bag, no charts, no car seat, no Max. And I couldn't hold the thoughts in my head.

"Bah!" Max shouted again.

I picked him up and carried him back to the living room. Dad was still standing by the window, his hands in his pockets, his shoulders hunched.

"You think Aunt Jean's home?" I asked. "If I called now. About this adoption agency."

"Probably." He held out his hands. "You want me to take the baby?"

"I've got him."

He nodded. "Sam. Whatever happens, things will turn out all right."

"I know," I said. I shifted Max closer against me, and I looked up at the ceiling, at the stars Mom had stuck up there for my birthday. I hoped Max's mom would think of stuff like that.

chapter twenty-four

THE PHONE CALL COMES when I'm at work. "Sam Pettigrew," I say.

I've been looking for a bug in the Kepler's guidance system, spending the past day and a half going over the old code, and it takes me a few minutes to readjust, it takes me a few minutes to realize what he's saying. "What?" I say, more sharply than I mean to.

He says it again. And then he's quiet. We're both quiet.

I hit escape. "How did you get this number?" is the only thing I can think to say.

"Your dad," he says.

I put my head in my hands. And finally we decide that Saturday will work out okay. This Saturday will be fine.

I spend most of the morning just kind of moving

MARGARET BECHARD

from room to room. I can't seem to settle in one place or concentrate on anything.

I'm sitting at the kitchen table, staring into a cup of cold coffee, when Sarah comes in. She puts her hands, lightly, on my shoulders. "I'm taking the girls over to your dad's."

"Okay," I say.

"He said something about trying your old waders on Abby."

I laugh and look up into her face. "Remind him that she's only five."

She squeezes my shoulders. Then she leans down, her face close to mine. "He'll like you, Sam. Don't worry about it," she whispers.

I nod, and she turns my head and kisses me, softly, on the lips.

I go outside to watch them leave, Abby and Meg waving from the back windows of the van. It's a beautiful day. The grass will need mowing soon. I go in the garage and stand there, staring at the junk we've accumulated. I should clean out this garage.

Instead I get out the fishing gear. Spread it out on the lawn. Check my reels and lines and poles.

A car pulls up in front of the house. A used Volvo. Good car. Safe car.

A kid gets out.

Eighteen years old. Eighteen years last November.

He comes walking up the driveway. He's tall and kind of skinny. Broad shoulders. Football player, maybe. Maybe hockey. Brittany's big blue eyes. Blond hair. Curly hair. He smiles as I set down my fishing pole.

"Hi," he says. He holds out his hand. "I'm Max."

MARGARET BECHARD says, "Once a week I volunteer in the nursery of a local high school, helping to care for the babies while their parents are in class. It began as a vague idea about research for a novel, but the fact is, I go because of the babies. There's nothing so gratifying as reducing someone to hysterical giggles simply by sticking out your tongue. After my stint, however, I am happy to come home to my teenage sons. Who may not laugh so hard when I stick out my tongue, but who, at least, do not wear diapers."

Ms. Bechard is the author of five novels for younger readers and one young adult novel, *If It Doesn't Kill You*, which was praised by *School Library Journal* for its "healthy doses of humor."

Margaret Bechard lives in Tigard, Oregon, with her family.

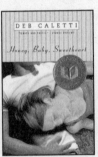